Rough Strife is

"so rich and affirmative, you'll want to read passages aloud to someone you love." —*Los Angeles Times Book Review*

"a novel that neither idealizes nor excoriates marriage....*Rough Strife* replaces 'and they lived happily ever after' with a real story." —*Newsweek*

"written with an irony and wit that one rejoices to find...it is a nearly perfect miniature: economical, compassionate, clear-eyed, wise." —*Los Angeles Herald Examiner*

"a brave and moving book." —*San Francisco Review of Books*

"an almost flawless anatomy of a flawed institution, an intelligent and robust account of a marriage that is like land's end: a post of earth divided again and again by rough seas that stand stubbornly whole when the tide recedes." —*Saturday Review*

"as satisfying to the intelligence as it is to the feelings. A very fine first novel." —*Kirkus Reviews*

"Lynne Sharon Schwartz registers the fluctuations of marital feeling with the fidelity of a Geiger counter. She understands the permanent resentments that can be mixed with love...and the alternating currents of weakness and strength that pass between people whose lives are joined together." —*New York Times Book Review*

Lynne Sharon Schwartz

ROUGH STRIFE

PERENNIAL LIBRARY

Harper & Row, Publishers

New York, Cambridge, Philadelphia, San Francisco
London, Mexico City, São Paulo, Singapore, Sydney

Portions of this work originally appeared in somewhat different form in the *Ontario Review, A Shout in the Street,* and *Weekend Magazine.*

Grateful acknowledgment is made for permission to reprint:

Quote from the "Food and Fashion" section by John Ciardi. Reprinted from *The New York Times.* © 1978 by The New York Times Company. Reprinted by permission.

Lyrics from "Some Enchanted Evening" by Richard Rodgers and Oscar Hammerstein II. Copyright © 1949 by Richard Rodgers and Oscar Hammerstein II. Copyright renewed, Williamson Music, Inc., owner of publication and allied rights throughout the Western Hemisphere and Japan. International copyright secured. All rights reserved. Used by permission.

First PERENNIAL LIBRARY edition published 1985.

Designer: Trish Parcell

Library of Congress Cataloging in Publication Data

Schwartz, Lynne Sharon.
  Rough strife.

  I. Title.
PZ4.S3997Ro 1980 [PS3569.C567] 813'.54 79–2740
ISBN 0-06-091282-0 (pbk.) 85 86 87 88 89 MPC 10 9 8 7 6 5 4 3 2 1

Thanks to Harry . . .

Now let us sport us while we may;
And now, like am'rous birds of prey . . .
. . . tear our pleasures with rough strife
Through the iron gates of life.
ANDREW MARVELL

Wasn't it miraculous, that she could feel this way after so long? Desire, she meant, and its fulfillment. Ivan lay collapsed on her, slipping out in a protracted slowness. She made no effort to keep him. In a moment she would open her eyes to the bedroom ceiling, an off-white marked by grainy, old imperfections of the surface. She would repossess identity, a structure chiseled by circumstance. Till then she would yield to this larger existence: the breadth of oceans, the reach of continents! A dupe, of course, yet what a fine geographical extravaganza, sponsored by Ivan. Caroline smiled.

He moved, and left her. They lay side by side for a while, till Ivan sat up and announced, "I have to go jogging."

Caroline sighed. "I suppose it's only fair that you should exercise other parts as well. Legs."

"It's heart and lungs, actually."

"I see. So you'll have taken care of the reproductive, circulatory and respiratory systems. Very thorough. Then you can come home and eat, for the digestive."

"Come on," he pleaded, and aimed a feinting blow at her jaw. She stretched flat so he could climb over her to get out of bed, and observed his body vaulting through space.

"I should be back in a half hour or so," he said, "I'll ring. Will you hear me?" How discreet he was, this lover. Decoded, the question meant, was she going to get up or go back to sleep? Ivan felt that too much of life's precious time was spent in sleep. He rang because he claimed the weight and jingle of keys would disturb the delicate euphoria of his jogging.

"I'll hear you. I'll be out of the shower by the time you're back."

Just the other day she had found some lines about love quoted in the morning paper. " 'Love,' " she had read to Ivan, who stood soberly before the glass pane of the china closet, holding his tie, " 'Love is the word used to label the sexual excitement of the young, the habituation of the middle-aged, and the mutual dependence of the old.' " She paused. "Is that what we have? Habituation?"

"We're still in the young category," Ivan said with a smile, his eyes, not his head, veering in her direction. A pleasant leer. Good. She didn't care for the writer's attitude anyway. She leered back and bit into her bread and cheese with a youthful appetite. Ivan flipped the long end of the royal blue tie over the short, pulled it up from under, and negotiated the knot with pained jerking motions of the neck, as though his head, dark and pensive, were striving to escape from captivity. He hated business clothes and maintained he would be most happy living in a loincloth, but he was going to meet with the sources of money. He was in a position of power at the Metropolitan Museum, where at last his particular virtues had found their niche: impeccable taste, a learned eye, and a brilliant, apparently artless diplomacy in regard to the sources of money. Watching the manoeuvres of the tie, Caroline thought impassively, He makes this sacrifice of comfort to earn our daily bread. She earned it too, but the higher mathematics could be taught in slacks and pullover, so innately elevated were they. Ivan worked his way into a suit jacket.

"Beautiful," she commented from the kitchen table. "They'll never guess you abhor the corporate structure."

He grimaced, ran a finger under his collar and left the room.

Were they? Were they really among the young?

She was out of the shower and halfway through her exercises when she realized Ivan was not back. He always came straight home after jogging since he was too sweaty to go anywhere else. She had never been possessive about his time—freedom was part of their tacit pact, their longevity. But she feared the dangers of the park, especially on deserted weekdays, gray mornings. It was a gray Tuesday. Ivan was on vacation and would have dismissed her fears as nonsense. Probably he had met a neighbor and been enticed into one of his errands of mercy, fixing warped keys for helpless children, pulling shopping carts up the street for elderly widows, sweat notwithstanding.

She forced her attention to the exercises, strenuous ballet warm-ups to keep her body young and pliant. (For whom? she occasionally wondered. Herself? Ivan? Some future imperative?) She had the notion that the exercises could hold back the incursions of time, as a disciplined army holds back a destructive horde. She also believed in the story of the boy who could lift a cow. He began the day it was born and lifted it daily. There could be no one day when she would wake up old and find it impossible to do the lifts and swings and balances she had done easily the day before. In Zeno's paradox, which boggled the minds of her freshmen, the arrow never reached its mark, the intermediate steps being an infinitely divisible succession. Speeding by, time moved in tiny increments. Caroline was forty-five, but as her friends sometimes told her and she believed, she looked years younger.

When she was finished she checked the kitchen clock. He had been gone more than an hour. Suddenly, overlaid on the clock's square face there came to her a vision of Ivan attacked on an abandoned lane by three swaggering boys with knives. That he carried no money enraged them; they cut him up and left him bleeding on the limp July grass. Transfixed, she reran the scene in greater detail. They approached him, skinny dark boys in dark clothes walking close together with their shoulders almost touching, and blocked his path. How poignant was Ivan's surprise, he who lacked the imagination of disaster. They surrounded him, pinned his arms back, felt his white shorts for money. When he tried to break away, as he surely would, they pulled out their knives and slashed at him: face, arms, chest. Few people walked down that lane; he would bleed to death, slowly. Or else be discovered and brought back to her breathing his last. Perhaps he would live on, an invalid. There was a man in the next building in a wheelchair. He stopped neighbors to tell jokes and they suffered his advances out of pity, for he had been mugged and was paralyzed as a result. The vision flashed again, Ivan lying on his back on the lonesome path, stretched out as if crucified, this time the front of his white shorts a bloody hole. Caroline pressed her fists to her eyes in a surge of self-hate. How could she even imagine such a thing? Dead would be better than that. For his own sake, she would rather have him brought back to her dead.

She shook herself as if to throw off a web. He disappeared, he had no sense of time; that was his way. Last summer he took the girls to the beach and didn't reappear till nine-thirty at night. She had pictured trawlers dragging the ocean floor for their bodies, if it was possible to drag ocean floors, especially in the dark. When they walked in, brown, sandy and laughing, she blanched as if at a trio of revenants. She had vowed that minute to waste no more of her ebbing vitality worrying over him. Very well, then. Back in the bedroom she pulled her jeans from a bottom drawer and tugged them up with satisfaction. You didn't have to run to stay young, she thought savagely as she reached for the hairbrush.

It was a terribly hot day. Just last week a neighbor, fifty-two, a mere couple of years older than Ivan, dropped down on the tennis court, stone dead, after three games in extreme heat. Precisely. Ivan was not the mugging-victim type: too big and arrogant. He might be sprawled in the same pose as Jeff Tate, felled by heat exhaustion and heart failure. She should have warned him not to go—Jeff's wife said she had warned him, not that it helped—but Caroline tried to avoid a wifely tone, even in middle age. That was part of their tacit pact too, never to adopt the mannerisms of "husband" and "wife." Besides, given the nature of Ivan, solicitude would evoke a contrary response. So out of their joint perversity, he was dead.

The children, away at camp! How could she possibly tell them? They were too young for such a loss—Greta a mere baby and Isabel nearly full-grown in body but a child still when it came to grief. Poor Greta—her first summer away. Ivan had been so devoted to them. When Isabel was small a glow surrounded the two of them, as if they were lovers. Then Greta was born, and he found he could be in love with two girls at once, the lithe pre-pubescent and the rosy infant. Caroline had had to accept the dispersion of his love. Isabel at fourteen pretended to a coolness she thought was mature; her grief would be enormous but restrained. Caroline would writhe inside with the need to see her weep.

Greta, transparent as glass, would be all tears and talk, defying any attempts at distraction. Caroline would look at her and see straight through to the shattered heart.

She laid down her hairbrush with a sharp bang. This was carrying the game too far. He would return safe. He had to. Fate might be cruel and thoughtless—her own life, God knows, had been buffeted by time and chance—but there were some things that simply could not be permitted to happen, even in fantasy: the suffering of children. . . . And yet it happened all the time, in real life. She herself had been barely older than Isabel when her mother died. She remembered the torment vividly, though she no longer felt it. Why should her children be exempt?

Sinking into the enveloping easy chair in the bedroom, she closed her eyes and recalled the odious packing ahead of her. They were setting off tomorrow for a three-week camping trip in Canada. A vision of cold mountain lakes and the soft splash of canoe paddles with an arc of droplets gleaming off their length transported her into a shaded green peace. This hour would be forgotten. Any second, Ivan would ring the bell. They would pack up, go to bed early, and rise at dawn to slip into their jaunty white car, its motor humming a promise of space and solitude. She jerked to her feet. The car! He had mentioned last night, just as she was falling asleep, that he needed to bring the car in this morning to have Angel look it over before the trip. He had forgotten to remind her as he left. Ah well, that was Ivan. Her relief was immediate, like an inner flood of light.

She ought to make sure, though. She approached Ivan's desk drawer with a faint sense of violation. They were very careful about privacy: regarding desk drawers, mail, telephone calls, a minimum of questions was asked. Discretion had helped them stay married. But this was different. She pulled open the drawer. The car keys lay there, splayed out like an open, three-fingered hand. Never mind, he must have taken her set again. Like a child, he liked using her things—towels, fountain pens, scissors, camera. She reached up to the high shelf where she kept them. Her fingertips touched the jagged edge of cold metal, and she fell back in the chair, numbed at this horrible betrayal by her own emotions, by life itself.

He had simply vanished, like Gauguin. She allowed the crazy notion to settle over her gently, like a blanket. Like someone dragging about with flu, who finally surrenders and goes to bed, she felt the relief of giving in. Yes, after all these years, and yes, in his white jogging shorts, idiotic as it seemed. He could always borrow clothes from his younger brother Vic, who was the same size and lived only a mile downtown. There was a streak of the unpredictable in Ivan; it was one of his charms. From the beginning, he had had the yearnings of pioneers, explorers, adventurers. He longed to discover landscapes and make them his own by striding through them and imprinting his foot. Were he living in another age he might have driven stakes into the ground or hoisted his country's flag. She, rooted to the spot, adventurous only within the confines of her self, was what held him back. Something within him had finally revolted.

Why, after all, should Ivan want to spend his entire life joined to her? He had thought at first that he would want to, but now he had changed his mind, and with good reason. She was difficult. Though no more so than he—their difficulties, alas, were perfectly complementary. And she was not astonishingly beautiful, nor brilliant (except in her own obscure and narrow work), nor even particularly kind. There was nothing spectacular about her. Though there had been moments, with him, when she felt spectacular, so illumined she might glow in the dark. But in truth even the common glow of youth had left her. Wasn't it true despite all the exercising, hadn't she seen but pretended not to, that in certain bends and twists the skin on the outside of her upper thighs crinkled like parchment? She squeezed her eyes shut in resistance. Of course she had seen, this morning, and the morning before, many mornings before, but she had made believe it was nothing, an accident of the light that could happen to anyone in those contorted positions. But it would not happen to Isabel, or to Isabel's taut friends. Ivan was a courtly lover; he would have pretended not to notice. He knew she could not forever remain as she was the day he first saw her. He had also grown abstracted— he might indeed not have noticed. Other men would. Eventually she would become like Blanche DuBois, making love only in the murky shade of lanterns.

This was no time for levity. She crouched deeper in the uncritical embrace of the chair, her arms huddled round herself though the room was warm. He was gone, then. She would have to accept it somehow. What she would never accept was his timing. Just after they made love— that was the most unkindest cut. Had he been planning it all along? This is the last time, baby, you better enjoy it! No, no, Ivan could not think like that. More likely it was with lordly benevolence, condescension. I grace you one last time . . .

It was not any failing in her that had decided him. He was quite aware of her flaws, and abundantly tolerant: they had both tolerated a great deal. What he could tolerate no longer was his own love of a flawed object. A secret perfectionist: not from her but from love, from his own vast and undiscriminating devotion, had he run in his white shorts and blue shoes, run out of the park to the tip of the island, across a bridge to the mainland, out to the hinterlands, out, out, away from love. Love the dark victor whom no one outwits, as a young poet said. Ivan would outwit it. At the very start, in Rome, he had tried to outwit it. He was more skilled now, at evasion. Oh yes, she could see it radiantly, tall broad Ivan against the flat morning horizon, running steady and swift towards a purer region.

Well, it was a pretty picture, but it could not soothe the fury pervading her like bloat. Who did he think he was, running out on her after so many years, running out on their children for some metaphysical indulgence? Had he coerced her into marriage, then, only to desert her? Had he weathered the strife of two decades only to leave now when they were more calm? Of Isabel and Greta she could not even think any more; a ring congealed around her heart at the unspoken sound of the names. Who did he think she was, to have spent years of her life accommodating him in more ways than she wished to remember, and then be left bereft in middle age, so that no one else could ever see her as she once was, in her beauty. And the perversity of him, to leave on the very eve of their vacation. All winter, through the grease fire in the oven and the breakdown of the plumbing, through Greta's broken arm, her own bitter fight for the Women's Studies program, the theft of the Volvo—through all the abominations they had dreamed of a time alone. He had made a mockery of their dream. Of their whole lives.

She felt tears coming, but she would not weep for him, the bastard. There had always been something elusive about him. Let him go, then. Let it all go. Comforting visions of her life without him sprang up like magic flowers, unfurling as she watched. She would have the bedroom all to herself. It would have Renaissance prints of her own choosing— nothing past 1650 except maybe Matisse—and not a plant in sight. With Ivan's crowds of plants, their living room was an alien green jungle, permeated with the smell of soil.

Flowers instead; fresh flowers every day, graceful and mortal, in wine flasks. At night she could finally sleep diagonally without the pressure of his palm on her spine, her shoulders, her ribs: seeking, touching. Always touching. Her clothes could overflow into the empty drawers, for she would gather up his socks and handkerchiefs and underwear, his plastic shirt stays and foreign coins and spare shoelaces, and throw it all away. Burn it. It was a pity they were not still living in the old house—she could have tossed the lot into the fireplace and watched his socks turn to ashes. The shirt stays would not burn, stupid little things, so out of date. But he liked relics. Suddenly she could see the tight impatience in Ivan's lips as he struggled to insert them, and her heart fell into an abyss, with an intimation of the frozen solitude preparing for her.

She refused it. She rejected it, shuddering. If only to defy him, she would not be solitary. There were opportunities, and she had by no means forgotten how to seize them. The world was full of them: the blond smiling man in the administration office whose eyes strafed her body crossing the room. And the one who owned the bookstore and always tried to detain her, showing her new texts. Even the young Greek in the pizzeria who twirled the dough so splendidly that it danced between his fingers. "You busy Saturday night, lady? You and me, we go dancing!" Well, no, not him. There were limits. But all the others: she would like to run her fingers down all those hairy chests.

She was relaxing in the chair, mildly dazed in her fantasies. Things of no substance. But Ivan was real! Her heart thumped once, so hard it left an ache in the bones of her chest. He had been gone two hours. He might really be in pain somewhere. Waiting, wondering why she didn't come. They always, always came to each other's aid, even in the worst of times. She rushed from the apartment and down the four flights of stairs.

In the lobby Mr. Abrey, the malcontent superintendent of the building, hacked at a broken mailbox with the handle of a screwdriver. She and Ivan had thought him sinister when they first moved to New York ten months ago, because he never smiled and spoke only to warn of various impending perils. But now for some reason, perhaps his mortality—he was dying of cancer—Caroline trusted him.

"Good morning, Mr. Abrey. You haven't seen my husband around, by any chance?"

"Why, off and left you at last?" His chuckle was like a rake dragged along concrete.

"He went out jogging a couple of hours ago. I thought maybe you'd seen him around the building." She swallowed hard her abandoned pride. Mr. Abrey would be dead soon anyway.

"Jogging. Ha! Run themselves into the ground. The park ain't what it used to be, either. They hide in the bushes and wait for people to come by. I ain't seen him." He coughed, spit into a handkerchief, and turned away to tap his screwdriver against the hollow metal of the box. His frame was wasted from disease and radiation treatments—x-rays, he called them. There were no contours discernible beneath the dingy gray of his work pants; the fabric hung as if suspended on bone. In the presence of a dying man her visions of disaster did not seem far-fetched at all. She stood a moment longer, mesmerized by Mr. Abrey's tapping and the mortifications of his flesh, then darted out the door, around moving cars and into the lonesome park.

An occasional jogger passed with a salute. They must take her for one of their legion, even without the uniform. Perhaps she could stop one and ask if he had seen a tall man in blue running shoes and white shorts. But their eyes were glazed and they stopped for nothing. After a few minutes she had to slow down to a walk. Ivan was nowhere, not on the path or the narrow shaded lanes branching off, nor lying in the clumps of trees beyond. No tire tracks from ambulance or police car. When Caroline finished her search there came the quiet satisfaction of obligations discharged. Nothing more could be expected of her. She walked slowly home. The truth was nothing, a gap; not crime, nor sudden illness, nor abandonment. Her mind, filled before with extravagant fancies, was hollowed out, as when a show of fireworks is scraped from the dome of the sky, leaving a black arc.

Back home, the bedroom was too light. It seemed night should have fallen, she had ranged through such vastnesses of time. But it was not quite one-thirty. She drew the shades. Sitting down in the soft chair, she let her head drop and her eyelids fall closed. In the darkness, the ordeal she had put herself through seemed gross, and inappropriate at her age. Was that love? She made herself recollect viscerally Ivan making love to her this morning, and was not surprised to be touched by longing. But the longing was remote. She could regard herself and her reflexive longing with a large, condescending indifference. Ivan had said their love was not the habituation of the middle-aged because they were still on the other side, in the sexual excitement of the young. Very likely he had been mistaken; very likely she had skipped right from the sexual excitement of the young to the pathetic dependence of the old, with never any relaxing habituation in between.

She must have fallen asleep. At the touch of his hand on her head she gasped and the breath stuck in her throat.

He was grinning. "Sleeping again. As soon as I go out, you sink into decadence."

He was unaltered save for the dripping sweat of exertion, while she felt years older, dry. "My God! Where the hell have you been? I thought you dropped dead or something. Why couldn't you call, at least?"

"You know I don't carry any change." He waved at the pocketless white front of his shorts.

"How did you get in?"

"I met Mr. Abrey out front. He told me you went out, so I borrowed his keys. What's the trouble?"

"What's the trouble! Didn't it occur to you I might be curious? I went out to look for you! I didn't know what became of you."

Ivan was quite calm. "I thought you would realize I had things to do. I brought the car in to Angel's, and I had to wait there. The carburetor's clogged. I have to go pick it up later."

"But you didn't even take the car keys."

"Oh. I met Vic running at the south end of the reservoir. So I figured, rather than come back home I would take his keys. He still had that spare set. Anyway, I stayed at Vic's awhile."

"But why couldn't you call me from there?"

"I didn't know the car would take so long. Come on, Caroline, you sound like the Spanish Inquisition." A private joke—she was expected to laugh on cue. Ivan reached for her hand but she folded her arms.

"How are things at Vic's?" she asked dully.

"Not so good. There's a problem with Cindy's leg. You remember that knee injury she had in the winter? It seems the bones didn't knit together properly. She's in a lot of pain. She'll probably need a leg brace or maybe an operation."

The intrusion of other people's troubles was revitalizing. "You know, it really kills me how you can walk in blithely after three hours and tell me all about the carburetor and Cindy's knee and whatnot. People don't just disappear like that, in shorts, dammit. Don't give me that crap about money. I'm sure Angel would have loaned you a dime—you're one of his best customers."

"Shut up!" he yelled. "Shut up!" A powerful assault of sound. What did he do with all that power, where did he keep it trapped, all the hours he was not shouting? "I will not have you keeping track of my comings and goings! I don't do it to you. I can remember days at a stretch when I barely saw you. If you have to worry, that's your business!"

He stopped short and gazed around the room blinking, as if he had stunned himself as well. The silence was heavy. At least she had left him notes, she thought, so that he knew she was alive. Ivan raised the shade and opened the window wide. He leaned out and looked over the park. "As a matter of fact," he said in an ordinary tone, turning to her once more, "I was concerned about Cindy, and then I was thinking about Greta and Isabel, away. What a risk it all is. I didn't think of calling you. I thought you were busy packing." He tossed the car keys over to the dresser. They struck the edge and landed at her feet. As Caroline picked them up and handed them to him their fingers touched; she pressed his.

"I'm concerned about Cindy too," she said quietly. "And you know I don't keep track. But Ivan. More than three hours just for a quick run around the park? I thought you were bleeding to death on the grass."

"This is sweat, not blood." He pulled her to her feet, beginning to smile. "Blood is red. Sweat is colorless. I jogged back from Angel's too. Feel." He grabbed her hand.

He knew she hated clammy clothes. Caroline tried to pull away but he held her wrist tightly, forcing her hand to his cold, wet shirt, where the sweat made a grayish arc on his chest. "Stop! You're disgusting," she cried, but she laughed. He had both her wrists in his hands; she struggled in vain.

"Come on, show some affection. Sweat is very good for you. You know you love it." He tried to force her arms around him, but she kicked and twisted in his grasp. They were laughing wildly, but suddenly Caroline went limp and silent.

"Let me be. I'm not in the mood," she said.

He released her and pulled the T-shirt off. "I'm going to take a shower."

"That's an excellent idea."

Ivan threw the wet shirt at her. She caught it in one hand and threw it back at his head. "Mr. Abrey said you probably left me at last."

"I wouldn't leave you right before we go camping. I'm scared to sleep in the woods all by myself." He picked up the shirt, rolled it in a ball and stalked off to the bathroom.

Only when she heard the steady stream of the shower did she feel full relief, a protean relief that took the eerie shapes of disappointment. What high drama it would have been: his funeral, her grief, the shock and sympathy of friends; or his hospital stay and her saintly nursing; or even his sudden abandonment and her rectitude in the face of despair. Now she would have the packing instead, while he attended to the carburetor. Drama indeed.

In fifteen minutes he was back, wearing the red kimono she bought him for their last anniversary. He was addicted to Japanese kimonos. When they wore out she bought him new ones, in vibrant colors. He had washed his hair too. She watched him brush it with rhythmic, energetic strokes. His father had told him, when he was a small boy, that if he brushed his hair vigorously twice a day he would never become bald, and Ivan still believed it. For as long as she had known him, over twenty years, morning and night he brushed his hair with unflagging vigor. No doubt he would brush it in the woods as well, outside their tent. And in fact his hair had thinned only a bit since the days of his youth. He must have felt her eyes on him, for he turned midstroke, caught her gaze and lowered his lids momentarily, as if in code. When he was quite finished brushing, he knelt down beside her chair. "My sins are washed away," he said.

She leaned forward and put her arms around his neck, and he rested his head on her lap.

"Move over." He got into the chair with her. She loosened the front of the red kimono.

"I thought for a while you had decided to disappear."

"What did you say?" he mumbled.

"I thought you had finally had it."

"Had what?"

"You know. With us, I mean."

"Don't be ridiculous." He was fumbling with her clothes. "Why are women's things constructed in such an infernal manner?"

"I should think you could manage by now, with all your experience. Let me do it."

"Much obliged." He kissed her. "You have strange lapses, you know, Caroline? If I didn't leave before, why would I now?"

"I don't know. I thought it, though. Don't you ever have fantasies like that, about me?"

It was pointless to ask such a question of Ivan. He never lied to her; he only abstained. Instead he moved his hands over her body, lovingly. It was not true that there was no progress. Progress seeped through as slowly and secretly as exposed wood darkened with age. Five years ago she

16

would have shouted much longer, and Ivan would have mocked her fears. There would have been days of gelid silence before they came close again. Now none of that had happened. All that had happened was that he had forced her to discover, one more time out of many, the great reaches of inner space. Just as she shifted in the chair to accommodate Ivan, she would accommodate the repetitions of the future.

Perhaps he noticed a wandering of her attention, for he opened his eyes and stared hard at her face, all of him concentrated and given to that gaze. Nothing elusive about him now. "You're not going to cry over this, are you?" he asked.

"Oh no," she replied. "Oh no, I don't cry so easily these days."

"These days? That's funny. I remember when I first saw you, you seemed pretty tough even then."

"Did I?" She laughed dryly. "Back then? That was nothing, Ivan."

His hand on her breast stopped moving, and he looked at her with a sad frown. "Am I that bad?"

"I didn't say that. No."

There had been a quiver of recognition when they first met. Not love at first sight, but bowing to destiny. Since then, periodically she would fall in love with him over again, and in cooler phases, knowing it would recur, anticipated it almost as some transcendent ordeal. Living with him, she had come to believe that men and women are given, or seek unawares, the experience they require for their own particular ignorance, that pain is not random. She thought often about Michelangelo's statues that they had seen years ago in Florence in the first excitement of their love, figures hidden in the block of stone, uncovered only by the artist's chipping away the excess, the superficial blur, till smooth and spare, the true shape is revealed. She and Ivan were hammer and chisel to each other.

"Well, you looked scary to me," he said. "Classy. Very sure of yourself."

"That was just the champagne."

" 'You may see a stranger,' " he sang, " 'across a crowded room.' "

She ran her fingers lightly over his lips. "Don't sing, love, please. The way you sing, you spoil everything. And anyway, it wasn't a crowded room. It was a crowded roof. I've told you a million times."

They met across a crowded roof, where the trappings of romance ensnared them. The occasion was a sunny June wedding in Rome in the late fifties. She was a friend of the bride, Ivan a friend of the groom. Cory and Joan, the nuptial pair, were later divorced, for intricate reasons, back in the States. Caroline and Ivan, for reasons no less intricate, endured.

Ivan and the bridegroom had Fulbrights; almost all the laughers and drinkers on the noisy crowded roof had Fulbrights, and with the Fulbright year drawing to a close, the party had an aura of ritual joy, consummating the year's friendships and leisurely labors. There was an accordionist, a short stocky man with glittering gray eyes and ruddy cheeks, who swerved among the clumps of wedding guests smiling beatifically, his belly gravid with the instrument that hung from thick straps on his shoulders. He was playing the most beautiful melody Caroline had ever heard. Or perhaps it just seemed the most beautiful. She was aware that it might be the champagne. Even the goblet seemed to refract the melody in its cut-glass surfaces, beaming flashes of red and blue and green in the sunlight. Intoxicating too were the red flowers in boxes lining the walls of the roof, the heady smells of cheese and sausage leavening the fragrant air, and the array of dresses, the filmy dresses of the women. She wore a shimmering romantic dress herself, lavender, a throwback to an older era, with ropes of beads and a pearl-gray garden party hat whose great brim hid most of her fair hair and shaded her inquisitive, stern, and rather fragile face. She felt she was masquerading. The accordion-ist's tune rose like a kite, then dipped, rose again and plunged. In the curve of every plunge, as in a kite, was the promise of the rise to come. The melody shifted from major to minor and back again, showing a touching faith, Caroline thought, in the recurrence of opposites: that the crooked would become straight and the broken mend. The tune must have a name, maybe even words; it came from somewhere. The little accordionist drew her like a Pied Piper. Carefully, she shaped a sentence of inquiry in her minimal Italian, and plucked the man by the sleeve.

"Scusi, ma come si chiama questa canzone?"

He bent his head towards her, adjusted his smile, and shrugged in the classic Mediterranean way, ambiguity ele-vated to an art. Then tipping an invisible hat, he receded, moving backwards through the crowd, facing her with a rueful smiling mouth, so sorry he couldn't explain. Puzzled, she turned to the panorama of tiled roofs below. Rome was a mosaic of segments of earth—amber, ochre and brown, the churches and the bridges spanning the somber river gray and white cutouts pasted on. Above, the sky hung flat and static, the artificial blue of postcards. She felt like throw-ing her head back and laughing, though why she should feel so happy she didn't know; she didn't know a soul at the party except Joan, the bride; didn't know a soul in Italy, for that matter. She was a stranger to everyone, and had recently buried her father in chilly dark New England earth. April in Massachusetts had been not only cruel but cold. An only child, she sat at his bedside during the prolonged illness whenever she could, stitching a needlepoint hanging from the hospital gift shop, later to be tossed out unfinished, the horse in the center incomplete. For weeks her life was circumscribed by his death, the four walls of the square hospital room, the four fibrous edges of the square hanging.

Finally he died. The cold, pebbly soil resisted the spades. The diggers struggled while she watched with her heart dulled, out of patience at last. Afterwards she bought herself this trip with the savings he left, like a treat for a child who has behaved exceptionally and unexpectedly well in a difficult situation. Good-natured Joan arranged for her to stay in the apartment of a nomadic Fulbright who was off in the south. Caroline was drunk on the unreality of it.

Turning back, she leaned against the low wall and surveyed the party. A quite tall man with darkish skin or a permanent suntan seemed to be looking at her, glowering almost, with concentrated feline eyes, above the heads of the crowd. His expression was strained, as though he couldn't make her out clearly, or couldn't remember where he knew her from. He did not smile, and he appeared solitary, distinct from the people surrounding him. His stare was so prolonged it might have been rude, except that it was utterly without hostility. An elegant stare. She could be mistaken; no doubt she was. He was squinting not at her but at the splendor behind her—history, *gloria mundi,* while she was only a particular young woman at a party in a romantic hat. As if on a dare, she winked at him. So faint, a mere twitch of the lid, he would never notice. The probability that he would, considering the distance between them, the number of people present, the faintness of the gesture and his state of readiness, was something infinitesimal, which she might attempt to calculate were she not high on champagne. Immediately he started towards her, clearing a path through the guests, moving with a sort of stealthy grace, all unaware. Aha, the noble savage approaches, thought Caroline. She drank some more, her eyes cast down.

"Hello. You winked," he said soberly, halfway between question and statement. He was less elegant, less finished, close up. Shirtsleeves rolled to the elbows, red tie hanging loose and askew, and longish hair mussed from the breeze, he might have been one of the broad-backed Roman stone-cutters in his Sunday best, out slumming among his social betters, proud and wary.

"I'm really not that sort of person at all," said Caroline. "I don't know what came over me. I didn't think you'd see from so far away."

"I have contacts."

"Contacts? Oh, contact lenses." She laughed and peered up at his face from beneath the brim of her hat. "I can't tell they're there."

"Of course not. That's the idea." His name was Ivan, he said. What was hers?

She hesitated. People of primitive tribes, she once read, do not give their names away; they cannot so readily entrust that emblem to strangers. Her name, too, seemed more than she could afford to give away to this large and sober person. He looked tenacious; she might never get it back. Besides, his eyes were peculiarly powerful, not from any supernatural glow but because they did not always focus accurately. When she thought he had been looking past her they saw her wink. And just now, while they gave the impression of profound penetration, Ivan was nodding to someone passing by. Only a fraction off—there must be a term for it in pathology—but it certainly gave him an air, and made her suspicious.

Still, this was a party and she could hardly refuse.

"Y-n or i-n-e?" he wanted to know.

"I-n-e. Why?"

"I don't know." He smiled for the first time. It changed his face. He became ingenuous, accessible. "I-n-e sounds more interesting, for some reason."

"Oh. Would you have lost interest in talking to me if I had said Y-n?"

"Almost nothing could make me lose interest in talking to you," he said in his serious manner, and then he smiled again, gallantly.

Caroline played with her beads. She was not used to such candor, or such flattery, so fast. But why "almost," then? What was the "almost"? And fast was the last word she would choose to describe him. He bore himself with uncommon calm, as if he issued from a leisurely, antique place off the beaten path, a place from which old-world gallantry might travel full circle to meet new-world frankness. She lifted her glass but it was empty.

Ivan led her over to the opposite edge of the roof, where a row of tables served as a bar. They passed the accordionist, once more playing the rare tune. He widened his eyes at Caroline and grinned as though they had a common, conspiratorial past. She edged past him in confusion.

The young Americans hovering around the bar in bright colors appeared flighty against the historical backdrop, out of their element, like mounted butterflies inspirited with life. Vulnerable, enthusiastic prey. A bunch was laughing and exclaiming over some kind of emblem hung from a hook on a pillar. Caroline had to stand on tiptoe to see past the shoulders of the young men guffawing. The thing was a fat carrot, point downward, with a tuft of green growth on top, flanked by two large round purple onions.

"What is that supposed to be?" she asked Ivan, and saw the instant the words left her tongue. It was bad enough that she had winked. Now he would think her not only forward but naïve, or else willfully provocative; easy game either way. Strangely, this prospect gave her a humming exhilaration.

Ivan glanced up at the vegetable object and glanced quickly away. "It's some kind of . . . uh . . . fertility symbol, you know. Maybe it's a tradition at Italian weddings." He cleared his throat and busied himself reading the labels of the champagne bottles.

Why, he is delicate, she thought. A man of taste. She smiled more freely as he finally handed her the glass. His party manners were perfect, as though acquired with diligence. "Rather blatant, wouldn't you say?"

"Oh, I don't know," he replied awkwardly. "It must be left over from some primitive rite. People used to be more matter-of-fact about these things than we are. A wedding, after all . . ." He stole another glance up at the fertility symbol. "Would you like something to eat?"

She couldn't help laughing out loud. "Oh no. Not right now, thanks." Not quite yet, anyway, she was drunkenly tempted to murmur. But no, not to Ivan. She had to respect his modesty. They walked away from the tables. "You must be one of the ubiquitous Fulbrights, is that right?" Caroline asked.

"Yes. You make us sound like a lepers' colony, though."

"I didn't mean to. What are you studying?"

"Something about the relation of architectural style to political regimes, the rise and fall of empires, and so forth. A narrow little study. What about you?"

"Oh, I'm not studying anything. I have no group or intellectual purpose. I'm on vacation. Between jobs, actually."

"When you're not on vacation or between jobs, what do you do?"

"Math."

"Math?" He stepped back. Caroline nodded. "Can you do statistics?" he asked with a kind of reverent disbelief.

She might easily have taken offense; it was a stupid question she had answered sharply enough in the past. But happy and vaguely excited by standing so close to him that their sleeves brushed when they raised their glasses at the same time, she gave Ivan a reprieve.

"Of course," she said smoothly. "I've tutored people in it. People in the social sciences or the arts, who need it for a project. People like you." She smiled.

He stared as before, ran his fingers nervously through his thick hair, and refocused his eyes on her. "Listen," he said softly, touching her wrist with two fingers, "if you're not busy tomorrow we could go to the Campidoglio. You know, the Capitol, where they got married today? I'll show you the wolf."

"Wolf? What wolf?"

He was a man to rely on. He promised a wolf and there was a wolf indeed, beneath the great hill of the Capitol. It was a golden afternoon with a glaring, overripe sun and clean dark shadows. Yesterday, alone, Caroline had followed the other wedding guests up the stairs to the grand piazza overlooking the city, where Michelangelo once scattered flagstones, dark and light, to make a mad checkerboard. Today Ivan led her away from the steps and off to the left. Though gentle, his grip on her arm was very firm. The side path he chose seemed to lead nowhere: shadows, bushes. She had a flash of crazy fear. Where was he taking her? Who was he, anyway? And why was she letting him pull her—yes, pull, for his fingers had tightened around her arm—off into the shadows? But in less than a minute they stood at the bars of a small murky cage dug out of natural rock. Their arrival roused the wolf, who sat still and attentive in a far corner. She lifted her head and bayed, an eerie sound reverberating off the stone. Ivan beamed proudly, as if he had conjured the entire scene.

"And I didn't believe you."

"I know." He grinned. "But it's full of unlikely things. You've only been here four days. You have a lot to see."

"Yes," she said, feeling suddenly weak. He made it sound overwhelming, like the ritual labors assigned in mythology. She wondered if he would be taking her on any more bizarre excursions, if he was planning to make her labors his own. Would they fetch golden apples from the ends of the earth?

"What's a wolf doing down here?"

"Remember Romulus and Remus?"

"Oh, those twins that were suckled by a wolf."

"Yes. Their mother sent them down the river in a basket, and the wolf rescued them and nurtured them. Later on they founded Rome. So this wolf commemorates the founding of the city."

"A wolf for a grandmother," said Caroline. "Without her, no Rome, no Empire, none of it."

"Great mother figure, you mean?"

"No, what I really meant was the idea of a beast as responsible for all of this."

Ivan laughed. "Behind every great civilization is a beast."

"Well, look at the ancient Romans, how beastly they were, all that murder and intrigue."

"But they were noble too. Remember all the noble Romans in Shakespeare?"

"Noble and beastly together? A neat trick. Look where they put it, though, right below the City Hall. Beneath law and order they hide this savage wolf, who keeps them alive on her milk."

The wolf, as if eavesdropping on its visitors, approached them from the rear of the cage. Glowering from slate-gray eyes that looked at once treacherous and ready to weep, it grasped the iron bars in its front paws and raised its gray-white muzzle up towards them, against the wire-mesh barrier. In that pose of supplication, or threat, the torso of paler gray, with rows of teats like hairy knobs, quivered with each intake of breath. The wolf appeared to be panting with rage. Caroline could see tiers of ribs below the fur; she could imagine the stripped carcass.

"He doesn't seem very glad we've come," said Ivan, resting his hand on her shoulder.

"She. It may just be her standard performance."

Staggering slightly on her hind legs, the wolf jerked her head back and opened her mouth so wide that the angle between her jaws could have spanned a human neck. The teeth, glistening rows of them, were sharpened to a fine point; Caroline could picture them descending cleanly into their prey. The pink tongue was curled in a tremulous arc. The throat undulated as the wolf swallowed, and then she gave out right in their faces a howl starting in the depths of her register, streaking its way up like a siren, and ending on an unresolved querulous note. Anguish, it seemed, and vast in its breadth. Caroline gasped at the sound. Ivan squeezed her shoulder.

Abruptly, the wolf dropped down to four legs and trotted calmly back to the corner of the cage. She had withdrawn into herself and no longer projected anything, like an actor reaching the wings, the character falling like a cape to reveal the person beneath, innocuous.

It was chilly down there in the shadows. They walked back along the path and turned to climb the stairs for the spectacular view from the high piazza.

The beast in him did not show itself for a long time. Caroline was baffled. Perhaps he was lacking something, or she was. She had come here for pleasure and now she suffered in the flesh from wanting him. Exasperated, she pondered whether his backwardness—if she could call backward something which had hardly demonstrated an existence—might be a mode of originality, a "line," a feat of abstinence designed to so impress her that it would be the more amply rewarded later, as in a fable. But she was no Puritan; brought up by Puritan parents, she had seen the hazards of that way early and averted them through force of will. She was unimpressed by abstinence and disliked fables where rewards were meted out with an unreal justice. Ivan could have whatever he asked of her at once, deserving or not.

On the trip over—a ship, chosen to stretch the crossing and unravel her nerves—the images of her father dying were fresh, superimposed on the line of the horizon as she sat alone on deck. She rallied her spirit with childish visions of the sensual goodies awaiting her now that she was cut loose—dark-skinned, white-toothed musical Latins escorting her about the city of legend, making ardent love to her in shuttered rooms, *povera orfana* that she now was, healing with their tongues all her wounds. Mother bears licking the cub into shape. But her time was taken up by Ivan, wining her and dining her, cheaply—Fulbrights were notoriously poor; she had money and offered, but women weren't allowed to pay. Morning and night he telephoned with intriguing plans: the beach at Fregene, the Pantheon, picnics at Ostia. . . . He was dark-skinned and white-toothed, and he sang, too, badly, mostly corny songs from musical comedies, and occasionally he hummed the wonderful tune that the accordionist played at Cory's and Joan's wedding. Only he did not make ardent love. Caroline waited, a child of her time after all. Her freedom went as far as accepting advances or fending them off; nothing else.

Instead he orated on the stones of Rome as they trod them. He walked her through the ruins of the Forum and showed off his Latin on the inscriptions. He had attended a special high school in New York for smart boys only, he told her in a rare mood of revelation, a school favored by the sons and grandsons of Jewish immigrants, like himself. Besides that, he was a Boy Scout, he informed her. Couldn't she tell? He could still recite the Boy Scout pledge, and did ("courteous, kind, reverent . . ."), while they drank wine thigh to thigh in a trattoria. He knew everything about the paintings and sculpture, the fountains and the architecture, and he perused her with the same tender, educated discrimination. He looked for structure and composition, he told her, harmony of the parts and general resonance. She saw a great deal of Rome, but a Rome filtered through Ivan: he stood between the world and her eyes, refining the particles of light. And he kissed her good night at her door two times: lips warm and slightly parted lingered on hers briefly with a feeling of misplaced nostalgia, as if he and she had been lovers long ago and their passion long past, a frenzy remembered rather than anticipated, and this kiss merely the remnant, a little dangerous, a little teasing, and a little false, yet so sweet. Then he moved his lips away with the regret of old war movies: late for the train that would carry him from her, to battle and maybe to his death. She asked him in for the euphemistic coffee, but he said no. He wished he could, but he had an early morning meeting at the Fulbright office—if he came in he knew he'd stay too late. Damn right, thought Caroline. Those kisses left her wobbly as a teen-ager as she gazed from her open window after his body in retreat down the narrowing Roman vista—a study in perspective, Ivan the vanishing point. Her fingertips tingled and her mouth hung open in a moronic droop until she realized and clamped it shut, furious.

It hurt her. She woke in the middle of the night, cold and alone and indignant. She pulled the covers close around her and huddled, then threw them off and reached for a cigarette. Inhaling with long deep breaths, she imagined them in her bed in every possible pose, his full lips open and smiling, his dark hair like an Indian's mussed and falling over his eyes, from which he had removed the non-contact lenses and which perused her as always, and she displayed everything, she didn't care, so long as he would. . . . He came closer to her. It had grown so very dark all around them. She felt the heat of his skin, and an unbearable excitement. With a start, she awoke again in the dark. The air had the nasty smell of abandoned, burnt-out butts. Luckily the cigarette, half-smoked, had died harmlessly in the ashtray. There was a dreadful restlessness under her skin, as if a layer of fine ash were sliding beneath the surface. She had to get up to fling herself about, dashing in and out of the three rooms and pausing finally at the windows in the bedroom which overlooked a small square. In the daytime sturdy women, their hair wound in buns, with aprons and string bags crossed in ceaseless procession from the dairy to the butcher to the tobacco shop. They nodded to each other with austere dignity, or else stopped for vigorous dialogues that from Caroline's window had an aura of high significance. The men, narrower and lighter on their feet, skimmed past the women like frisky motorboats skimming past steamers or barges, saluting with admiration, a touch of awe, and a whimsical recognition of difference. But now in the small hours the square was still and dark; one wrought-iron street lamp with a diminutive gargoyle at the top shone a faint yellow light on the stone walls. Every few moments a Fiat, a toy car, bumped along the cobblestones with a clatter unnatural for the hush of night. Only three windows in the buildings around the square were lit: for celebration, sorrow, conspiracy, love?

"Don't you ever work?"

Ivan, leaning back with his eyes closed, lids against glass, laughed and shook his head. "I work going around like this."

They were sitting in a small angle of shade on the Spanish Steps, near a flower stand. The mingled aromas wafted through the hot air in sickening ripples. Caroline wiped her face with a handkerchief she had just dipped in a fountain when they emerged from the dead heat of Keats's house at the top of the stairs. On the way out of Keats's house their bodies had brushed and Ivan's mouth touched her hair. Maybe it was an accident, but she wished he wouldn't touch her if he didn't really want her, if they were only stray Americans going about together.

The slow-moving people in the square below were licking ice cream cones. She closed her eyes and conjured: cold, wet, sweet and vanilla melted on her tongue. Since she was a child she had done this. When her mother took away her ragged blanket she learned to fall asleep clutching a fantasy. The ice cream was cooling as it slid down her throat. Sweat dripped from Ivan's temple to his jaw, from his jaw to his shirt. She tasted that in secret too, running her lips over the angle of the jaw, feeling the roughness of skin on her tongue.

"I mean for your Fulbright project. Don't you have to do a paper, or an outline, or something?"

"Nothing much." He smiled. "A very general outline. Mostly we're on the honor system."

"That's a good deal you people get. At my job I had to come up with results all the time. Evidence of activity."

"I wish work didn't have to be like that," said Ivan. "I wish I could support myself someday doing exactly what I like. I mean, by some miraculous coincidence doing exactly what I like would be my work."

"What sort of work would it be?"

"Oh, I don't know how to say it. I've never really said these things out loud." He laughed and looked down at the square. "Not political science or history or the sort of thing I've been trained to do. I think I would be good at telling people how to go about getting what they want. That's if they know what they want to begin with." Ivan paused, as if what he was hearing was new to him. "I would like to figure out strategies—it wouldn't matter what field they were in. I would need to know just enough about the content to shape the strategy. It would be like an abstract design, but purposeful. Does that make any sense?"

"Sure."

"People would come to me with their ideas and dreams, and I would figure out a way for them to be realized." He laughed again, shyly. "Then I could do it for towns and countries and continents, and then I could be God."

"I see," she said. "Well, a little ambition never hurt anyone. Tell me, do you lie awake nights figuring out strategies to get what you want?"

"Oh no. I'm not a Machiavelli. But I have tried to do pretty much what I like, on a small scale. So far, anyway. Haven't you? That's the way I thought of you that first time, when you winked."

I didn't wink, she longed to object, but couldn't. "I've done what I had to, what needed to be done. Sometimes I liked it, not always. Even now, I can't always do as I like."

"Why not?"

She laughed without pleasure. "Because, Ivan, sometimes what I'd like to do just isn't done."

"Such as?"

"I don't think I want to elaborate. After all, we're really strangers."

"Are we?" asked Ivan, peering at her in surprise.

"I would say so," she replied coolly. "I would say you have kept us strangers. Strategically, maybe."

That was all, she decided. With that she had come more than halfway, if being met halfway was what he required.

He was honest enough not to protest. "Let's walk," he said with a sigh, and got up. Out of instinct and habit she watched his long body uncurl, a procedure invariably complex and beautiful. Then she remembered and turned away.

"You see those people coming around the corner licking their cones?" he asked. "I can't stand it any more. I must have some. The place can't be far."

Licking their cones, they walked together slowly toward cooler air. They were nearing the river.

"There's something I've been wanting to say to you," began Caroline. "I hope you won't be hurt, or think I haven't enjoyed all the things we've done, because I have. It's simply that . . . I really did just get here. I need some time to myself. To wander around a bit, on my own."

"I had a feeling you were working up to this."

"You did?"

"Yes, I can read your mind. Oh no, it's nothing mystical. I can see it on your face. I knew you wanted ice cream. I bet you never played cards. You wouldn't have a chance, even with all your math. Everything you think is written right there."

"I certainly hope that isn't so. And anyway, I can play chess."

"Well, I can't." He bit aggressively into the cracker of the cone. "Okay, when did you want me to disappear?"

"Come on, Ivan, I didn't say it like that."

"It amounts to the same thing, however you say it. So, when did you intend this moratorium to begin?"

Watching him attack the cone with feral motions, she was suffused with irritation. "Soon, maybe. Maybe right after we finish our cones. For a few days."

"It's your script, baby. Whatever you say. What do you call a few days?"

She stared. So he could talk that way too. A stripping away of civility to show the nakedness beneath, or the opposite, a cloak of brashness. Either way he tantalized. Were she an intimate of his she would hear such strange and jarring notes, atonal music. She would know him in his nakedness and in his masquerades.

"Do you want to call me on Friday?" she asked, suddenly frightened. It was Tuesday.

"If that's what you want."

They reached the breezy promenade along the river and stood facing each other like adversaries, each with a hand resting on the balustrade high above the water. Caroline had thrown away the empty tip of her cone but Ivan was eating to the very bottom.

"You could work on your outline," she said with a faint laugh.

"Don't tell me how to spend my time."

"Sorry."

They moved a step farther apart. The breeze gathered force, blowing their hair in their faces. Caroline's full skirt whipped about her legs. The sun was descending for a cool evening. Already, passing women spread dark knitted shawls about their shoulders. A red-haired boy speeded by on a bicycle, nearly grazing them. As they each drew back the boy bared his teeth and laughed devilishly.

All at once, with a shake of the shoulders like casting out evil spirits, Ivan recovered his good humor. He moved toward her. "It's too bad you're doing this right now, because actually, I was planning to ask if you'd like to come over for a drink."

"Were you?"

34

"Yes," Ivan said. "Come on, I'll show you my place."

Caroline's cheeks smarted, red in the wind. What had rushed through her as desire was molten rage. So he took it as a challenge. Well, she would not have him that way. No, love was not love that crept out of hiding through threats or ultimatums. If they were to duel, let it be with the grace of swords, with swoops and lunges, not the fists and hatchets of gladiators.

"I'm not in the mood any more. Your timing is off."

"Oh, do you require everything perfectly measured out and timed, everyone lined up like horses at the starting gate, mathematically precise? I don't know, then, whether I can . . . run in your track." It was not even sarcasm; he was soft-voiced as ever, and smiling straight at her. There was a proper lunge. And she might have negotiated a worthy response, might even have smiled back and conciliated, except Ivan had sliced so near the bone, his thrust slipping right into the groove of old wounds, of others who said the same thing—only not as succinctly and never on such short acquaintance. How did he know? Undeniably, he had contacts—he had warned her the minute they met.

In pain and shock, with all the civility of stomping fists, she muttered, "You wanted the last word, you had it," and walked off quickly, her head bent against the wind. Tears clamored behind her eyes but she wouldn't let them out.

She set out aimless and free the next day, Ivan's absence from her side a palpable relief. His long legs kept an almost martial pace, while she liked to amble. She could look now, or ignore, with unaided eyes; childishly she prized her ignorance simply because it was her own. She walked along the river again. Surely she could appreciate what a river had to offer without his refinement of vision. Today the water was black with a salacious tinge of green toward its banks, and sluggish, as befitted a river that had witnessed so much human intransigence. Against the flat milky sky jutted the castellations of an old fort where Renaissance Popes had fled for their lives. She didn't need Ivan to find that out: the stories were right in her guidebook. With Ivan she wasn't permitted to display a guidebook.

She stared her fill in the windows of expensive shops. Ivan, with fingers that could circle her arm, had dragged her from shop windows. He scorned the consumer economy and had a dread of being taken for a tourist. During the year he had bought ready-made clothes in Roman department stores, and with his dark hair and coloring he could easily pass for a native. How he loved to examine the menu in a restaurant and cast a nonchalant, compatriotic glance at the waiter, a tableau inevitably ruined when he opened his mouth to order. Harmless vanity.

She was an unabashed alien. She tried on dresses in an overpriced boutique on the via Frattina and ate in a place where waiters in red bolero jackets guarded the door with napkins over their arms. Ivan wouldn't be caught dead here, she thought slyly as one of them pulled out her chair. All day she played tourist—a relief to assume so general and commonplace an identity—and hours later, coming home, she smiled at the children on her square, who ran about in summer darkness till the moon was high, then yawned, sallow-cheeked, in the morning. Into her dreams crept parochial images of ruins, pasta and anchovies and coins shimmering inanely at the bottom of fountains.

When she woke she wondered, still in the thickness of sleep, what she and Ivan would do today. She raised herself to her elbows. Through the half-open shutters the blue trapezoid of sky was lit with dusty gold sunshine. There would be no Ivan today, she remembered, maybe never. She herself had dismissed him, in a fit of perversity or pique. No, pride. The *p*'s of those brittle words popped at her insolently like mockers. The day was a sightseer's delight, but Caroline was her specific self once again, set afloat like a lone particle in space. Queasy, she drank tea in sidewalk cafés. She shivered in the sun, grew dizzy walking in the Borghese Gardens, and finally, in the square of St. Peter's, tilting her head back to look at the dome, was hit straight in the exposed, tender throat by panic like a six-foot wave.

She sat down on a bench, relieved that it had risen and crested. For she knew panic; once visible and labeled, it could take its finite course. When she was fifteen years old she came home from school to find her mother lying on the couch in the living room. Day after day. It was strange to see. She had always been energetic, buoyed up by a life devoted to propriety at home and good works abroad. But now she simply lay on the couch. At the beginning she would read, then she would listen to the radio, and then she did nothing. Caroline started cooking without being asked. She took over the laundry in the evening and the shopping on Saturdays. Her father was silently grateful, withdrawn, possibly embarrassed. He was a prim man who taught earth sciences at the Milton Academy; his mind was safely fixed on inanimate rocks of arcane stratified ages. Even then, Caroline understood that the fleshly present was almost more than he could bear, and she sometimes marveled that she had been conceived at all. So no one spoke the name of the illness; it was a house where unpleasant things were never spoken out loud. She was sorry for her mother, and kind, but as far as she knew, sickness was a passing thing; there were no ugly symptoms, and there were pills. Surely she would get up again soon, the swishing, clicking noises of her fine administration would return. Caroline's attention was elsewhere.

She had become enchanted by mathematics, a Minotaur's cave of proliferating abstraction whose paths led to ever vaster but more intricately divided spaces, world without end. In excitement, she pursued the vanishing thread. The teachers gave her special projects because she had gone through the textbooks on her own, over the summer. They sent her to hermetic volumes on dusty back shelves, books about Fourier's Series, books with lushly complicated repeating patterns and sine curves that set up corresponding undulations of excitement in her head. One special teacher took her aside and initiated her into the secrets of spherical geometry, where—wonder of wonders—parallel lines met, on the rounded surface of the earth. And then, late Friday and Saturday nights, on the very couch where her mother's strength leaked out afternoons, the editor of the school paper, a slim talkative boy of astounding verbal agility, took off his plain silver-rimmed glasses to reveal liquidy blue eyes, slipped a hand under her sweater and under her skirt while her parents lay chaste and dreaming upstairs, and went home leaving her flushed and wakeful, tossing irritably in the dark. There was plenty to claim her imagination.

But one day she experienced a flash of knowledge of the kind that seems to come from nowhere, from the empty cavities of the body, yet has come from everywhere. And immediately from being a flash it congeals into the most obvious truth, the essential truth, around which our lives will bind themselves thenceforth like scar tissue around a wound. She knelt beside the couch where her mother slept and saw that the color of her skin was cement, and her yellow hair was no longer springy but sagging; even her eyelids and her lips had tiny wrinkles, and her cold hands were colder than ever. She shook her; it was urgent that her mother wake and acknowledge her, Caroline. The eyes opened with reluctance. In them, before they fixed on place and time and Caroline kneeling, was the knowledge. Quite plainly, Caroline saw death, which was no more than a soft, pleading terror coating her mother's eyes. It was not the terror that was so painful to see but the softness.

"What's the matter?" her mother asked. "You're staring at me."

She broke her stare. "Nothing. How are you? Do you need anything?" But she wanted to burst out in shamed laughter, as if she had said a gross and stupid thing. What could she fetch her now that would make any difference? That stern shape was going away from her. Looking closely, she saw that her mother was much thinner, thinning out every day, discarding cells like cargo from a sinking ship, removing herself gradually to lessen the shock. Going, going, gone—evaporating like a movie ghost. Being a lady in the eyes of her neighbors and teaching a daughter to be the same had been a consuming vocation. And now she was consumed. By sixteen Caroline was gritty; she had thought her mother's era of usefulness was over. She had even finished rebelling against her severity of outlook, and they had made a tenuous peace. Yet senselessly, as though she were an infant, it suddenly appeared that all rightness and balance came from the skeletal figure on the couch. Losing her, she would be adrift.

So it was that she became acquainted with panic, living with it nine months. For as long as it takes to make a baby, she labored to free herself of her mother. At the end she had the illusion that her labors enabled her mother to die. And she herself was delivered as well, of her panic. So that years later when her father's eyes softened over with terror, she could suffer the panic to abide in her for as long as it took. And the bearing of it and the ridding herself of it came easier, like a second baby.

But Ivan! A stranger, no blood tie, what had he ever

done for her or given her that the loss of him should be such an ordeal? Some accomplishment, she groaned. Some love, to be distinguished by the degree of pain it could cause. She despised people who doted on the sources of their misery.

When night fell she bought a loaf of bread and a liter of wine to take upstairs, and she sat on the floor trying to drink herself to sleep. There was not even a radio, and the square below was inexplicably quiet. "They have all gone into the world of light," she murmured, and slipped naked into bed. Now, what had he found repellent about her? In the dim light from out the window she touched her face with her hands as if something grotesque might have sprouted there without her knowledge, as if she might resemble the small gargoyle thrusting from the solitary lamp-post below. She did not imagine love, or Ivan's body against hers. What she needed seemed, monstrously, to have gone beyond the consummations of touch. She wanted to be enveloped even more thoroughly, obliterated. She wanted to subside to something he could carry hidden in his flesh like a mother kangaroo. These images filled her with self-disgust. In a fury she bolted upright and threw a pillow across the room. She had a powerful arm. It hit the half-filled wineglass, which fell over and shattered. As in a Jewish wedding, she thought bitterly. He had shattered the glass by proxy. Her innocence gone, the temple destroyed. She had been pierced by the cruel, mocking shafts of love.

He called the next morning. She leaped from sleep to the phone, to bask in the voice coming at her like pure warmth. His voice had a low, narrow range and a huskiness at the edges that might break into a laugh at any moment.

"Well, can you?"

"I'm sorry. Could you—I didn't hear what you said." Her cheeks flushed.

But Ivan said sharply, "Are you alone?"

Aha! She could see his dark head pulled back warily, his pupils crouching behind the lenses. Was she alone! She had barely a living relative.

"What do you think? At this hour, God! What time is it?"

"Eight-thirty. I'm sorry I woke you. Cory and Joan are having a party tonight. A sort of farewell. Joan tried to get you all day yesterday. Where've you been?"

Caroline leaned back in bed, crossed her legs and began to smile. She would have him yet; she could almost feel him on the tips of her fingers. "Out."

"Well, anyway, do you want to come?" he went on. "About nine. We could have dinner first."

"Sure. I don't have any pressing engagements. But listen, Ivan—" She paused, shocked at herself, and plunged on. "Before I see you again I have to tell you something."

"Well?"

"Okay. I had a really bad day yesterday, and I'd like to know . . . is this a—a love affair or what? I'm not the subtle type. I need to know what's going on." Again she colored, but he couldn't see her.

There was a wait. "What do you want it to be?"

"I asked you first."

"Well, I should think it was obvious, what I want."

"Obvious! It's not obvious at all," she cried. "If that's your idea of obvious I'd like to see what you think is confusing. If anything is obvious, it's that you don't know what you want."

"This is something we should discuss in person." She could hear his relief, and even a tinge of jubilation. The laugh was poised and ready to break out. Conniving lazy bastard. She would have him, all right, but she had had all the labor of it.

"Caroline." It was a voice that could tease like a probing finger. A shiver rose through her. "Are you still there?"

"I'm here."

"Do you have your haughty look on, you know, your Greta Garbo look?"

"You're vile."

"Ah. I've wondered," he said cheerfully, "what sort of sweet nothings you'd murmur."

"I'm not at that point yet."

"Believe me, I'm not taking anything for granted."

"Oh, please," she cried, "let's not start all over again. This could go on forever, till we're too old."

"You're right. I submit."

"I don't want you to submit," she cried even louder. "I want you to . . . want."

"I want, goddammit. Is that what you want to hear? I want. I want." It was the first time she had heard him so angry. His anger was hard, like varnished wood.

"But what are you mad about? Is it so awful to say that?"

"I guess it is. For me."

"Well, I'm glad you called, anyhow."

"I could come over right now, and bring you breakfast."

"No," she said quickly, looking at the broken glass, the stained rug. "I have to straighten up the apartment and take a bath."

"Oh, I'm not fussy," said Ivan.

"No." She laughed. "I want you to suffer." She might as well laugh, if that was how he was going to be. He was funny, after all.

The party was supposed to be held on the roof where they had met, but a heavy gray sky foreboded rain, so it was held in the apartment below, Joan's until Cory moved in. Caroline and Ivan walked there, singing, from the restaurant. They had drunk a good deal at dinner. As he pressed the door buzzer, Ivan slipped his fingers inside the waistband of her skirt; she retorted that he was fresh, and they were laughing like fools as Cory opened the door.

"Come on in," he said. "I see you two are already in the party spirit."

"Saluti," said Caroline, stepping in and pulling Ivan after her. Raising an imaginary glass, she looked around. "Do you still keep your vegetable genitals hanging up? They were hung so well."

Cory paled. He was a blond, cherubic young man, younger than Ivan; as in poetry, the roses fled from his cheeks. Ivan soothed him, then moving on, he placed Caroline against a wall, leaned up close and kissed her. "You frighten people," he whispered, grinning with a kind of pride.

"But do I frighten you? That is the question."

"Not in that way, no."

"How, then?"

"I'll tell you later."

He released her and walked into the crowd. As she followed, she marveled that they were here at all, in this fragile ambience of transients having a last fling. Why were they not back in her place, since that was all they could think of anyway? Ivan brought a piece of pungent cheese to her mouth. She opened her lips, he slipped it between her teeth and she understood why. Weeks of tantalizing. It was all part of the act, an extended prologue, and Ivan a lavish, leisurely producer, a Cecil B. De Mille of the boudoir. "My vegetable love should grow vaster than empires, and more slow." Never had she encountered a virtuoso in the prolonging of desire: mostly they were eager to prove themselves at consummation. An uncommon lover, possibly, but also uncommonly reluctant. She touched his leg surreptitiously and he brushed her shoulder with his in response.

"Let me introduce you to some people," he said.

They joined a man and two women on paisley-covered mattresses near a window. The man, Ed, had a Fulbright to study art history. He was lanky and boyish, with unruly pale brown hair and skin as smooth as a girl's. Next to him sat an older woman, plump and bouncy, and opposite, his wife, Rusty.

"It was every bit as bad as I thought it would be, having it in a Catholic hospital," Rusty said in a toneless voice. She was gaunt, with deep shadows under her eyes, thick brown braids, and buck teeth. Ed poured more white wine into her empty tumbler, which she clutched so tightly that her knuckles showed white. "The nuns wouldn't give me a thing for the pain. They just stood there, three of them, standing over me yelling, *'Spingere, spingere.'* "

Caroline looked questioningly at Ivan.

"Push," he whispered in her ear, lingering an extra second on the final, breathy sound.

"But it was finally all right, apparently?" said the older woman, Sarah.

"I pushed. What else could I do?" She moved her stunned eyes to the face of each listener in turn, as though they could offer alternatives. "But those nuns had no feeling. If something went wrong they would let me die—I kept thinking that the whole time I was pushing. It was horrible." She tipped her head back and downed the wine. "I hated all of them, and Ed and the baby too."

"How old is the baby now?" Caroline asked.

"Five weeks."

She examined Rusty more closely for signs of damage. She was skinny on top, and the rest of her body was hidden by her long skirt as she sat cross-legged on the mattress.

"We thought of bringing him along to show him off," said Ed. "We have a basket. But at the last minute we realized it would be pretty noisy here, so we left him home."

"You don't mean you left him alone?" Sarah asked.

"Sure. We do it all the time."

"You can't do that," she cried. "You can't leave a five-week-old baby alone in an apartment all night!"

"Our neighbor would hear if he cried," said Rusty, waving her thin arm through the air. "I'm there all day. I have to get out at night."

"Don't you realize what could happen!" Sarah rose to her feet excitedly. Strands of auburn hair slipped from the bun at the top of her head. "Crib death. Fire. Burglars. He could even choke from crying. I don't understand you two. You must go home right away."

Ed patted his beardless jaw. "I don't know, Rusty, maybe . . ."

"Nonsense. He sleeps straight through the night. He's a marvelous baby. And he has his pacifier."

"He could choke on his pacifier," said Caroline without thinking, then she put her fingers to her lips. She was the stranger; they were all friends.

"I can't believe this. I mean, we've been doing this ever since he was born. Times have changed."

"Babies haven't changed, and you've been damn lucky," said Sarah. "Listen, I'm going over there. Give me a key. I can't sit still another minute knowing that baby's alone. Bob? Bob?" She elbowed through the crowd to find her husband.

"I guess we ought to go with her," said Ed.

"Jewish mothers," Rusty grumbled. She stood up, smoothed down her skirt on her jutting hipbones and stalked off, setting her empty glass on the window sill. The window was wide open; Ivan removed the glass.

Caroline looked at him. "I'm not keen on babies myself, but really . . ."

Ivan turned to her absent-mindedly, desire forgotten, and laid his hand on her arm in a simple, friendly gesture. "It's scary, isn't it, to have a baby at all?"

"Nobody has to do it if they don't feel up to it." She shrugged. "Joan and Cory seem happy, don't they?"

"I don't know. They look the same to me."

Later, when they were leaving, Ivan wanted to drive around to all seven hills of Rome. The views at night, he told her, were spectacular. They went from crest to crest. Beautiful as Ivan promised, the city drifted below, black and starry. But back in the taxi after the fourth hill, Caroline reached out and put her hand on his knee, and he leaned forward and gave the driver her address. They were silent the rest of the way, and as she pushed open the heavy, recalcitrant door.

"Here we are," she announced foolishly. Ivan moved to the center of the room, where he gazed around, sullen and helpless like a juvenile offender ushered into his cell.

"Is that where you sleep?" He gestured to the old gray couch piled with books and newspapers.

"No, there's a bedroom. Over there."

He came to her. He suddenly seemed very much a stranger—there was something demented about taking him inside her. Her yearning fled, leaving her vacant, chilled and a bit shaky. This was all a big mistake, but it was not too late. She could apologize and ask him to leave: she had reconsidered and it would not work out. She heard herself say softly, "Are you going to tell me now what you're so afraid of?"

"Please," Ivan said, shaking his head as if in pain. "I don't want to talk now." He lowered his lids and nodded toward the bedroom, giving her a slight nudge. Chivalrous even in this poignant urgency, he wished her to precede him through the bedroom door, and so she did.

"Well," Caroline said right after, lying next to him and breathing hard. "I thought maybe you weren't interested. Or you couldn't do it."

"What's the big deal?" asked Ivan. "Anybody can do it."

"Not like . . ."

He chuckled, looking the other way. As she chuckled, she remembered, alone in her room after she won a spelling bee. A solitary, proud glee.

"You're not a wolf," said Caroline. "You certainly took your time. A real gentleman."

"I'm a wolf in sheep's clothing."

She looked him over. "You're certainly hairy enough. You must be the black sheep."

"Actually, in my family I probably am. Drifter. Can't stick to anything. Tell me, do you think I'd make a good gigolo?"

She laughed. "She'd have to be a strong old lady. What's your family like?"

"Poor but honest," he said. "Not now, though, all right? Now come over here. Please. That time was mostly a relief. Maybe we could . . . get to know each other?"

She moved closer. He took her hand and studied it, touched each finger and joint and brought the palm up to his lips. "We'll begin at the extremities," he said, "and work our way inward."

"You're lovely," said Caroline. "But you're not a foot fetishist, are you?"

"Oh, shush. Keep still and let yourself be worshipped."

" 'An age at least to every part.' Is that what you have in mind?"

"It's not a bad idea."

"Ivan, you're such a romantic. I never dreamed—"

"Well, what of it?"

"It's perfectly all right. Sensitive, aren't you? Go on, get on with it. Then I'll do it to you."

She woke late. Sun streamed in through the slits of the shutters. Slanting bars striped the north wall, and in the flat parallel beams of intruding light, motes of dust drifted. She had her back to Ivan but felt he was awake. When she turned, his eyes were fixed on her, greener than she had ever seen them, and squinting.

"Where are your contact lenses?"

"On the dresser."

"Do you make love with them in?"

"I can. It makes no difference."

"Did you?"

"I suppose so. Yes, I got up later and took them out, after you fell asleep. What is this, the Spanish Inquisition?"

"I'm always in a rotten mood in the morning."

"I'll fix that. Good morning." He circled an arm around her and pushed his leg between hers.

"Don't. I don't like that approach."

Ivan moved away. "What's the matter. Did something happen?"

"No, everything is fine. I'm getting up. I want to go to the bathroom and then make some coffee."

"Will you come back after?"

They had coffee and rolls together in bed, and then he put his arms around her and kissed her. The touch was overpowering, and the impulse to sink against him unwanted and beyond control. Her body was no longer her own, nor, as in tales of passion, was it his. It was some lush, willful alien that knew only craving and brutish pursuit of what it craved. She began to weep.

"What is it?" he cried. "What the hell is going on?"

She wiped her eyes on the pillowcase. "You made me

ask. You wanted to see if you could get me to ask for it. How long it would take you. So now you see. Now you can go home and pat yourself on the back. It's humiliating, that's all."

Ivan lay without moving, his face impassive. "I don't understand how you can say those things," he replied at last. "It's ridiculous. You're assuming things that have no basis."

"Oh, you're so innocent, aren't you? I see the type you are now. You don't act like a brute, no, you don't act like a boss, but you manoeuvre and manipulate. It comes to the same thing. Oh, you must love to see women wanting you—you are attractive, I admit. Some kind of operator."

Ivan gave a dry, callous laugh. "You flatter me." He pulled his arms close to his body, gripping one wrist tight. As he closed his eyes Caroline thought she saw his lids tremble, and was horrified. She touched his shoulder, but he had moved far beyond reach.

"Ivan," she whispered. "I'm sorry. I hurt you. Maybe I was wrong. Tell me."

"I have nothing to tell."

"Tell me how I'm mistaken. I'll believe you if you just say it."

"You remind me of King Lear," he said, opening his eyes. His voice was lighter; there was even the faintest trace of the edge of his laugh. "You want to hear how much? A lot, okay? I didn't want to start something with you, because . . ."

"Well, why?"

"Because I could tell . . . I had a feeling that if I did, I'd have to go on doing it for the rest of my life." He smiled ruefully. "Thumping on and on, sort of . . . fucking my life away on a woman."

Caroline laughed. "But I'm not one of those insatiable types. I never thought . . . Do I seem like . . . like that?"

"You don't understand. It's not what you would want," he said impatiently. "It's what I would want." He turned from her and shielded his face with his arm.

"Oh, God. I am sorry." She tugged at his shoulder till finally he turned back to her. "This must be what happens when people are in love."

"Oh, are we in love?"

"Yes," said Caroline. "We love each other."

"All right then, that's settled. So let's not talk about it any more. Now, how about it?"

"There's just one thing," she said later, as Ivan lay with his head resting on her stomach. "If you were afraid to start this, I mean, if you weren't sure you wanted to risk it, then why did you?"

He moved up and bent over her face. His eyes were very green again and very amused as he brushed the flopping hair off his forehead. He was trying to keep from smiling. "You asked, Caroline, remember? You said yourself I was a gentleman. I couldn't refuse a lady."

"Oh, you!" she cried, and lunged for him with hands like claws. But he was so much bigger, he had her pinned down in an instant, and he laughed at her squirming efforts to free herself. She didn't want to give in by laughing too, so her only defense was to close her eyes and simply feel him there.

She had never been given to having close friends. (Nor had he, he protested when she told him that, as if she had insinuated a secret, shameful weakness in him; she was his exception.) Growing up, she cared for math and music and chess, which endeared her to neither the arty nor the domesticated girls. Friendships with boys were not in fashion, so she got used to keeping her own counsel. She had never traveled in a pack, never learned how to make accommodations of the subtle, intimate sort. At college she roomed alone. She was agreeable and had friends, but they had to knock on her door and wait for her to open it.

How come, then, after so short a spell, she gave Ivan a key? She didn't understand it. She didn't understand herself any more. At the age of twenty-three it outraged her to suspect that lust could have so great a dominion. That was a comical concept and a comical word, not one you used in the ordinary course of life. "Desire" was what you called it, if you had to call it something. Lust: when she whispered it aloud to herself in the dark of night it had an ancient, quaint and scary hiss. More amusing than frightening, but she was frightened nonetheless. Never had she been so much under the influence of another person. The phrase itself suggested something shoddy and disreputable, as when her mother used to remark archly from time to time that the butcher seemed "under the influence." "He'd better watch his knife," she would add. Caroline, who took things literally, still remembered holding her breath and watching the steel of the cleaver flash as it tore into the raw red meat.

In college she had known men, and in the two years after, while she went to graduate school evenings and worked days for a firm of consulting economists. She understood little of their work, only the figures, which at the beginning she manipulated quickly with a richly joyous abandon, till she grew bored, and realized that statistics and computations would never keep her interest over a lifetime. She went through the men quickly too, and began to suspect that she manipulated them as well, though with an abandon less rich and less joyous. Always she felt driven more by curiosity than by passion or affection. Who were they, the students and economists, the lawyer and the actor? What were they beneath the clothes, the face, the patter? Strictly speaking, she supposed, a few of them plumbed her depths, physical depths she regarded without mysticism. But it was she who did the exotic spelunking. In fantasy she bored a hole in their foreheads and crept through the crannies of the brain to its visceral reaches, till a narrow shaft of light showed through. She came out the other end and dropped them. They were all too easy, a short trip, no lodes of treasure. A couple said she was callous; so what? Let them soften her if they could.

She had never lived with any of them, either. Sometimes she woke to the feel of their muscular legs twined with hers in the bed, not always a pleasant surprise, but she had never been so entwined that any could say to her as Ivan now did, "Where do you want to eat tonight?" or, "Let's rent a car for the weekend," or, "Do you want to go to a movie with Cory and Joan?" Cory and Joan, she thought wryly. Cory and Joan were only married, like thousands of other ordinary people, while she and Ivan were yoked together like animals in harness—flexible as elastic, true, but as hard to break. And it would surely leave telltale marks on the skin.

She was not the only one who had misgivings. The stout *portiera* of Ivan's building eyed Caroline with rancor and disapproval. Signora Daveglio dressed in black and always wore a striped apron tied around her waist. She had a wide clear brow and a tight mouth; horn-rimmed spectacles and gray-streaked hair gathered in a knot gave her an ascetic air. During the day she was most often found indoors on her knees, not in piety but scrubbing the steps of the building with a pail and brush. Her tenants grew accustomed to stepping around her and her pail, as well as to her penetrating stare directed at their backs as they proceeded up or down, away from her crouching form. In the evening she sat outside on a folding chair, her large feet in men's slippers planted squarely on the pavement, and read from beginning to end *l'Unità,* the Communist newspaper, holding it fully opened in front of her face like a book. On cool evenings she wore over her black dress a long green knit cardigan with a white stripe around the neck and down the center of the front; across the back stretched the word "Starlets" in white satin script, and above the left breast, in much smaller letters, "Diana." She said it had been sent to her by relatives in New Jersey.

Walking past the pail, Caroline could feel the stare boring into her back like twin rays of condemning fire. There was an oddly personal note in Signora Daveglio's disapproval, as though Caroline's evident willingness tainted all the members of their sex with disgrace. Her attitude toward Ivan was stern also, but more tolerant, as one excuses little children for bed-wetting, but not bigger ones, who should know better and whose offenses become a public nuisance. Caroline complained to Ivan, so one day he paused, before stepping over the pail, to greet Signora Daveglio, astonishingly, with the smile of an accomplished charmer, and presented Caroline as his *fidanzata.* The woman smiled back with relief. She wiped her fingers on her striped apron and shook their hands, regarding them as warmly as her stony features would allow.

"So I'm your fiancée now, eh?" Caroline said as soon as they entered the apartment.

"Well, you wanted her to stop looking at you that way. Anyhow, what's wrong with that? Isn't it a possibility?"

"I don't believe what I'm hearing. Are you suggesting marriage? The unregenerate independent spirit?"

"Oh, forget it. Are you hungry?" said Ivan, retreating to the refrigerator. But later on he brought up the subject again.

"I don't know what to say," she answered him. "I didn't

have marriage in mind at all. I came here for a good time."

"But aren't you having a good time?"

She sighed, lying in his arms. "Yes. That's not what I meant. Marriage doesn't strike me as a good time."

"You don't want to live in sin," he said. "You lose on income taxes. You have trouble with leases. You'll get your Ph.D. and try to get teaching jobs in colleges, and they'll spread nasty rumors about your private life. And what about the children? You don't want little bastards, do you?"

"Who said anything about children? I'm afraid of having them. I want to work with abstract concepts all my life. That's what I enjoy. Incidentally, you seem to know an awful lot about joint occupancy."

"I'm not interested in children right now, either. But we might change our minds, you know. You could wake up one day with a yearning in your bosom, Caroline. Right here. Or a longing in your womb. Right about here. An emptiness. A longing to be filled."

"You don't even know where anything is in a woman," she said, and moved his hand. "A longing to be filled over there would mean hunger. Anyhow, I'm not sure we're so well-suited. You can't go by this. This is not ordinary life, Ivan. This is a dream."

"There's never any guarantee. Listen, baby, I'm not going to beg. Excuse me." He reached over her to pick up the stack of *Daily American*s alongside the bed. Sitting up, he began leafing through the back pages.

She would not read a newspaper with him naked in bed beside her. Not yet, anyway. But Ivan, at the mere mention of marriage, behaved like a husband.

She put her arms around him from the back. "Why can't we just go on like this?"

"Because my money is running out. I have to go back

in a few weeks and look for a job. Caroline, please, I'm trying to find a certain ad."

"What ad?"

"For a used motorbike."

"You never told me you were planning to buy a motorbike. Do you think it pays, for only a few weeks?"

"It's not for me," he said tersely. "It's for Cory." Cory and Joan were staying on till winter.

"Oh," she said, and moved away. They even sounded married. The space between them felt cold, and Ivan very far. He would not like it if she touched him now. Did marriage confer rights? Did it mean you held bodies in common like so much jointly owned property? Ivan guarded his separateness. Once, watching him undress, she said as a joke, "It's wonderful. And it's all mine!" He had raised his eyebrows. "Mine," he corrected. And just as well, Caroline thought. That left her to herself too. But this feeling now of hesitating to touch made her sad, and nostalgic, as if the best of life, its richest flowering, were past.

She regarded his head, dark, large-featured, and meditative, as if she had truly attempted to bore through and failed. If she stayed with him she would fail continually; that would be her life's work. Maybe he could be peeled instead, in layers like an artichoke, till she reached the heart. Gobble that up and toss away the tough leaves and the chaff. But no, this one was something you might have to break to discover—a coconut, irregular and smooth; hard and dangerous and of manifold possibility, with a sweet pungent liquid concealed in the center, a nourishing milk like a mother's.

She might never get to the mother's milk. His talk was clever and off-center like his eyes, and most often a running companion to the instant, as if words were marginal to life; the past he put aside as soon as it became past. She knew very little about him, in the way of facts. If she probed he would tell her concisely what he thought, but not how. A mystery. Silent, his body spoke; the vocabulary of his touch was formidable.

She turned away from him. In a few moments she heard paper being carefully torn, then the stack of *Daily American*s was tossed to the floor and Ivan's arms were around her. "Let's be friends," he said.

She let him. For her, things were left too unsettled; she could not make love in such disorder. Her mother could never cook in a messy kitchen, either. The counters had to be cleared, the floor swept clean, the dishes from the last meal put away before the next was begun. She let him, as tired wives must sometimes let, she thought, offering little encouragement but no hindrance. He did it in silence and uncertainty. She felt for the first time the hardness of the floor in her lower back. Ivan believed in living simply, like a Quaker or a hermit. His bed was a lumpy mattress on the floor. When he was finished he gave her a hurt and puzzled look. Though she liked to pretend otherwise, she couldn't tell whether he was wearing his lenses or not. He did not ask what was wrong and she volunteered nothing.

He poured two glasses of wine and handed her one, then put his clothes on. Caroline watched, enthralled by the way he brushed his coarse thick hair in front of the mirror, with long vigorous strokes back and forth like a farmer swinging a scythe through a field of billowy black wheat. Her back still ached slightly. After a while she wrapped herself in his red satin kimono and went to look out the window. The Japanese kimono, taleggio cheese, expensive coffee, Piranesi prints and custom-made leather sandals were a few of the exceptions he permitted himself while living the simple life.

Out the window the natural light was fading and soft

street lights, house lights, and the garish yellow lights from across the square were coming on. A door opened below and Caroline saw the white horse with its keeper emerge for the evening. The horse was sleek and bare except for its halter, trimmed with two red pompons near the ears.

"The horse is out," she said without turning around.

"Already?" Ivan came to look, standing behind her, still brushing his hair. One tuft stood out stiffly, as if infused with an electric current. She touched it and it fell. "Don't you love me any more?" he murmured in her ear.

"Oh, Ivan," she said hastily. "Of course I do. But this is a fairy tale." She gestured down to where the white horse paraded smartly with its costumed leader.

"We won't get like everyone else. I know it. I want to be sure you're there."

"You're pushing me. . . ."

The horse stood on its hind legs and cavorted in a circle, a little mocking dance. Ivan gave a heavy-hearted sigh. "Let's go out and eat."

"Do you want to eat there for once?" She nodded again towards the square, the horse.

He laughed. "Are you kidding?"

Ivan lived on a small square opposite a large restaurant called La Taverna Romanaccia. On a huge wooden sign hanging over the door the name was painted in fat bulging script that had a wobble, as if a jolly drunk had guided the brush. Every evening at about six o'clock three lean and gawky boys dressed in tuxedos carried out round tables and lined them up in the square. They laid checked cloths and set out tear-shaped citronella lamps. As dusk fell, the beautiful and immense white horse came out a side door and was led around and around the square by a short smiling man in Renaissance garments: a green and gold satin tunic puffed out at the upper arms and below the waist, mustard-colored tights, a scabbard hanging from the wide belt, high-heeled boots and a broad-brimmed tufted hat. Ivan called him the Renaissance man, and said he wished he could have his job, even though he wasn't fond of horses—he wanted the costume. The Renaissance man and the horse paraded around the square till midnight, attracting tourists, Americans mostly, portly men in lightweight gray suits and women in pastels and white shoes; many of them patted the horse. As the early tourists filed in, music began, accordion music that could be heard in Ivan's second-floor apartment. Every half hour or so it grew loud and full, when the accordionist came outside to play for the tables on the square. He played Italian tunes Americans liked to hear, like "O Sole Mio" and "Funiculi Funicula," and an occasional melody from *The Barber of Seville* or *Don Giovanni.* Often when the tourists left, satiated, the men sluggish and the women languid, they gave a few coins to the Renaissance man. Ivan claimed he didn't mind the noise and constant movement. His rent was cheap; many people would not put up with Romanaccia. In fact, he confessed, he loved it, corny as it was: the sign, the waiters dashing with steaming trays held high, the horse, the Renaissance man, the accordion. Purely as spectacle, of course. He would never eat there. He ate in small quiet restaurants where real Italians ate. Way past midnight, after La Taverna Romanaccia closed, while the gawky boys rolled up the checked cloths and carried in the tables and the citronella lamps, the Renaissance man in gray work pants and a smock came out and swept up the horseshit.

Caroline took off the kimono and got dressed to go out. Downstairs, Signora Daveglio, on her folding chair and in her green club sweater, oblivious to the horse, the Renaissance man, the early tourists and the music, nodded at them from behind *l'Unità.*

"*Bello, vero?*" she commented unexpectedly, lifting her

face to the heavens in surprised, almost grudging gratitude. The weather was indeed fine, crisp and cloudless. Signora Daveglio was often surprised at favorable weather. She nodded once again, abstractly, as if to commend the infrequent but welcome rightness of things. Ivan and Caroline proceeded across the square.

"Do you hear that?" Caroline stopped in the middle.

"What?"

"The accordion." It was the tune from Cory's and Joan's wedding, the one with no name and no history, that climbed and plummeted like a kite in the wind. She could go in and ask; maybe this musician would tell her what it was. Except she didn't want to know any more. Why pin it down, assign it a local habitation and a name? Let it be whatever it was, only let her hear it. It had every possibility, a wondrous, luscious tune. At least for the accordion, she amended, and for Rome and for summer.

They traveled for two weeks in a rented car to see the smaller cities north of Rome. In Arezzo they got sick and lay groaning in a hotel room for three days, while every few hours a boy in knickers brought them up tea. But in Lucca they felt restored. In gray weather Lucca had a muted, ancient splendor; they loved it as a shared dream. Through the steady, soft rainfall they walked on Lucca's broad medieval walls and looked out over a mild hilly terrain. They went in and out of churches on cobblestoned streets to listen to the glorious singing, for it was a saint's day, the festival of Sant'Anna, and Caroline's birthday as well. She was twenty-four.

"Time you were married," Ivan said back in the hotel room at night, raising his glass in a toast.

"It's usually women who are so keen on getting married. Men are supposed to feel trapped."

"I felt trapped when I met you; marriage is merely a formality," said Ivan.

"What a charming thing to say." Caroline sat in a straight, stiff chair near the door, across from Ivan, folding her arms into the wide secretive sleeves of his kimono.

"Why don't you come over here?" His pose on the bed recalled Michelangelo's *Dusk,* which they had just seen in Florence, brooding and menacing but seductive.

"Because you distract me."

"From what?"

"From thinking."

"What is there to think about? It's almost time to go to bed."

"Marriage is very intimate, Ivan. You take a person to be your family."

He stroked his jaw and nodded sagely. "You fear intimacy. I see."

"I don't know a thing about you. You come out of nowhere, with no . . . no references, nothing. I have to take you completely on faith. What did you do over the past five years? What did you live on? You might have been married before. You might have children somewhere. You might have been in jail, or been a drug addict, who knows?"

"You know none of that is true. You just want to have everything spelled out before you make a new move, like a series of equations. All right, listen carefully, I'll give you my résumé: I was never married, I have no children that I'm aware of, I was never in jail. I've worked as a reporter, and for a while I put up houses for rich people on the beach, but I quit both and went back to graduate school. I've fooled around enough with girlfriends. I don't want to have to carry my hairbrush around late at night any more. I want to share the pots and pans and the food that's in them."

"It sounds like I'm incidental. I came along at the right time."

"I never asked anyone else."

She was silent for a while. "I don't even know your right age. Remember, the day we saw the wolf, you told me you were a well-preserved sixty?" She smiled unwillingly, remembering that day.

"I was born in 1928."

Typical. Like those authors in school they used to call "difficult," everything he said required a collaborative effort. "You're twenty-nine."

"What a deduction," he muttered. "Oh, but that's your field. I forgot." He took his book from the night table, Suetonius on the Roman emperors.

"Don't read!" she said sharply. "I'm trying to talk to you."

"I'll read if I want to. I've said all I have to say on this subject. And don't give me orders, either."

She watched him coldly. He turned a page and suddenly raised his head. "I'm sorry," he said. "I didn't mean to snap. Listen, Caroline, do you want to fight or—" He hesitated, glancing down at his book. "Or do you want to make love?"

"Fight or fuck, you mean. Isn't that what you were starting to say?"

"Okay. Fight or fuck. You win."

"Why can't you say it, then? You think you can't say what you want in front of a lady? Say anything you damn please. If we're going to be married we have to be frank, don't we? Uninhibited?"

Ivan groaned wearily. "I wish they had a TV. That's the trouble with Europe, not enough TV."

"Fight or fuck. Well, well. Is that the whole range of choices?"

He focused on her narrowly. "Maybe you're right, Caroline. Seriously, I mean. This just might not work out. We have such . . . differences. Maybe we should forget about it, after we get back to Rome."

"Oh no!" she cried, and rushed over to him. "Oh, please don't say things like that. Of course it will work. This"—and she waved her arm at the straight-backed chair near the door, as if she had left there her perverse pleasure in dispute along with his maddening resistance—"all this is nothing. Nothing," she repeated in a light, almost playful tone.

"It may be nothing, but I don't enjoy it and you do. That's the kind of difference I mean." He was searching her face acutely. It was essential to win him back. She used the most primitive methods there were.

Later she spoke into the still air. "Ivan?" He might be asleep, but something alert in his stillness made her doubt it. She nudged him. "You said you fooled around enough. But what if I haven't?"

His lips parted drowsily. "So do it later. Let me sleep." His voice was thick with grogginess.

"Do you mean to say you're giving me the . . . the . . . ?"

"Oh, for Chrissake, Caroline." He sat up. "I'm not giving you anything. It's all yours. Have a little imagination. You're so literal."

She had heard that before. It was probably what drove her to mathematics in school, where the clarities of Euclid could reach across centuries with nothing lost in translation; solutions were right or wrong and propositions were binding. Then as in any discipline, as she advanced it mellowed, and ambiguity slithered in. Euclid was expanded upon: deeper questions arose. Everything changed when you looked at it in three dimensions, four dimensions, in the context of the world and of time. But even so. Even so, in mathematics ambiguity, no matter how prolonged, was always regarded as a temporary state of affairs. The prospect of life with Ivan frightened her.

Worse than literal, she was crude. One day her indelicate poking would mortally wound his discretion and he would not want to live with her any more. She watched him trying to sleep again. His hair, mussed and unstylishly long, and his soft vulnerable lips were precious and ephemeral, and she suffered a premonition of loss, like a piercing pain in the throat. What was it Molly Bloom said? well as well him as another. But she also said she liked Bloom because he understood or felt what a woman is. Did Ivan? It was too soon to tell. Not yet, probably. But he had possibilities.

"All right," she murmured, stroking his hair. "I'll use my imagination." Most men nowadays, back home at any rate, had ugly crew cuts. She began to weave a tiny braid at the back of his neck. "It's possible we might be very happy."

"Happiness is not the point."

Had his tone been oracular or pompous she would have laughed out loud. It was sleepily casual, however, and took so much for granted that she wondered what was the point. But she couldn't be so unimaginative as to ask right now.

"What are you doing to me?" He jerked away and felt the back of his head. The tiny braid stuck out, wiry and stiff. Caroline laughed as he tried to untwine it. Inept at women's work, he tackled her instead, pummeling, and bit her shoulder gently. She bit back.

"Hey!" Ivan cried out in pain. When they compared bites, it was found she had unintentionally drawn blood.

"You see?" he said. "That proves that even though I'm physically more powerful I'm not the dangerous one. It's you we have to watch out for."

Ivan and Caroline didn't mind that it rained continuously for a week—it was a warm light drizzle that gave a shine and a haze of romance to the architectural wonders they set out to see—but Signora Daveglio, polishing the mailboxes in the hall on the damp afternoon of their return, was plainly offended by the weather. Her black umbrella, closed in limp folds, stood in a corner of the vestibule, dripping in uneven rhythms on a pile of obsolete copies of *l'Unità*. Her greeting was a grunt and a displeased tilt of her chin skyward.

"*Dunque,*" she pronounced at last, magisterial with hands on hips. "*Già sposati?*"

"What is it?" Caroline whispered to Ivan as he shook his head no, with that smile again, the smile of the irresponsible but irresistible rake, which as far as she knew he used exclusively on Signora Daveglio and which never failed to placate her.

"She wants to know if we went away to get married."

"Oh." Caroline lowered her eyes. Now Signora Daveglio would stare at her again, not so much with disapproval—she was too far gone for that—as with pity and scorn.

"*Ebbè . . .*" said the *portiera,* shrugging philosophically. She spread her palms and gazed at the ceiling as if to query, with Lenin, What is to be done? "*A Roma è stato un brutto periodo,*" she informed Ivan.

"*Anche a Lucca,*" he responded, and led Caroline off toward the stairs.

"What's that, a *brutto periodo?*" she asked at his door.

"A nasty spell. An ugly period, literally. She was talking about the weather."

"Ugly spell. *Brutto periodo.* That's nice. It has a nice

sound." It was comforting somehow. Only a spell, then bad weather passes.

They married. After the ceremony and the festive dinner with Ivan's lingering Fulbright friends, they walked hand in hand through the dark warm streets. "I guess I'll have to take you to meet the family now," said Ivan.

"Well, I should hope so. Did you think you'd keep me hidden away, like a secret vice?" She hesitated and let go of his hand. "How much will they mind that I'm not Jewish?"

"Not a lot. And however much it is, they won't show it to you. But believe me, they'll probably feel nothing so much as relief when they see you."

"Why do you say that? What did you bring home before?"

"No one. That's the point." He laughed. "They must think I'm not interested, like you did, or that I can't do it. Or else they have awful visions."

"Still, I'm afraid they'll mind. They'll think I'm, I don't know, an alien. Or suspect, at least."

"No," he said sadly. "They've forgotten their own history. My grandparents wanted American children and they got them, with a vengeance. My mother and father were born in America. They became like the people around them. They're the aliens."

His quick pace slackened and his face was closed to her; he was withdrawn to some remote, hollow recess, a place within that her burrowing might never reach.

"And you, Ivan? Will you mind? You've never even mentioned it."

"Caroline," he said, in a tone that made her feel stupid for asking, "it's not anything missing in you, so how could I mind? I only mind what's missing in me."

That was distantly chilling, beyond any help she could give. She took his arm and said, "Well, you got what you wanted, anyhow. We got married." But the words sounded strained and foolish.

"Yes. Now that that's taken care of, we can get on with our lives."

After that remark she didn't feel like speaking to him for hours.

In warm mid-September she met Ivan's parents, who lived in a modest suburban tract house in White Plains. Ivan had not grown up there but in lower Manhattan; he didn't care for the new house, he told her on the way up. Not that he wasn't glad his parents could finally afford it, but it had no history for him. No Depression had taken place there, no street fights, no rationing lines during the war. And he did seem a stranger as he shut the screen door behind him, sent his trained eye over the living room furnished in bland colors and predictable lines, and edged slowly into the low-ceilinged space. His parents were built the way he was, large and straight. His father was totally bald and benign, with a gruff voice and an overeager manner, as if he wished personally to ensure the welfare of anyone under his roof. Ivan looked more like his mother, who was dark, with strong features, and whose thick glasses hid pensive eyes. After the embraces and exclamations, to which she gave herself with zeal, Ivan's mother hovered nervously like a shy gray gull, then fled to the kitchen. Caroline followed to help serve the dinner. Ivan's mother turned from the stove to clasp her hands warmly. "We're glad to have you in our family." Her voice held an unmistakable note of relief.

"Thank you," said Caroline. Perhaps she was supposed to say she was glad to be in their family, but she was not ready yet to go that far.

"Ivan tells us you have no family of your own," she went on, spooning yellow rice into a bowl.

"A couple of aunts and uncles, that's all. I hardly know my cousins—they're all in Chicago."

"Well, I hope you'll consider us your family, Caroline. I really mean that."

"Thank you."

"Ivan has always had good taste. He had excellent taste in everything he picked out—clothes, pictures, everything. I remember, even as a boy he would rather do without than take something shoddy." His mother smiled. "I see his taste hasn't failed him."

"That's very kind of you. Thank you."

"Well, I don't want to embarrass you, dear. Now why don't you take this rice into the dining room and then come back and I'll let you carry in the vegetables."

She set the rice bowl on the table, which had a centerpiece of white chrysanthemums in their honor, and wondered how it would feel had she been raised in this family. Would she need to re-create herself in isolation, like Ivan?

"The only one missing from this gathering is Vic," said Ivan's father as he carved the roast. He carved with skill, and the roast was perfectly done, pink in the center and brown at the edges. "You'll meet Vic when he comes in for Christmas. Or maybe he'll come for Thanksgiving. We don't know yet."

"Oh, yes, I've heard a lot about him." This was not exactly true. She had heard of his existence, that he was five years younger than Ivan, and that he was going to law school in California.

"He wanted to come in for this occasion," Ivan's mother said, "but the term just started and they make them work so hard." She frowned with pity. "He felt terrible that he couldn't make it. He's going to call later on. It's three hours earlier there, you know. I told him to wait until about nine o'clock, our time. He says he spends all his spare time studying." She sighed. "I guess you can't get anywhere in this world without hard work."

"Yes, he's quite an individual," Ivan's father said. He gave his wife the first slice of roast beef and reached for Caroline's plate. "Here you go, Caroline. No danger of starvation tonight. Yes, both of our sons are real individuals. Summa cum laude at City College, both of them. And now one going to a fine law school, the other a Fulbright scholar." He reached over and patted Ivan on the back. "We're very proud."

"Come on, Dad. Cut it out."

"Why, what's wrong with a man being proud of his family?" He smiled broadly at Caroline. "I've been running a hardware business all my life, but I wanted to see them do something better. Just wait, both of you, till you have a family of your own. Then you'll know what I'm talking about."

"Now tell us all about your impressions of Italy," Ivan's mother said, raising her fork delicately. "How did you happen to meet each other?"

When the phone rang at five after nine, Ivan leaped up and dashed to the kitchen to get it. "Hey, Victor, how's it going? Hey, yeah!" he shouted, startling Caroline with his heartiness but not his parents, who beamed in rapt pleasure. "Yes, I'm back all right. . . . Yes, I finally did it. . . . Thanks. . . . Oh, great. . . . Terrific." He laughed insinuatingly. The three of them sat listening to Ivan's voice, alien and cheery, booming through the kitchen door. Caroline wanted to start a conversation but couldn't think of a subject. Any subject would be an interruption.

"I'll have to show you my slides. Say, I hear you're really doing great out there. How do you like it? . . . I didn't think you had it in you. . . . No no, only kidding. Listen, do you want to speak to the folks?"

They took turns talking to Vic. Both his mother and his father told him that Ivan's wife was a very lovely girl. "Come in for Thanksgiving and see for yourself," his father said. "Your turn now, Caroline." He waved the receiver at her. "Come on, don't be shy. It's all in the family now."

"Hello?" she said tentatively.

"Well hello there!" It was a low voice remarkably like Ivan's, but lacking his subtlety. The others surrounded her, watching. "I'm sure you feel kind of awkward," the voice went on, "but I just want to tell you I'm glad to have you in the family, and I'm looking forward to meeting you. Rumor has it that you're really terrific."

"Well, thank you very much. I've heard good things about you too."

"I hope my big brother's treating you all right so far?"

"So far, yes." She laughed. "Well, I think . . . I think Ivan wants to talk to you again. It's been good talking to you."

"So . . ." Ivan's father said as they returned to the living room, with brandy. "Where are you kids thinking of settling down? Or haven't you thought about it yet?"

"I hope I never settle down," said Ivan. "That isn't one of my goals in life."

"You know what your father means, Ivan," said his mother. "You've got to live somewhere. And you must have given some thought to finding a job? It's only natural that we should want to know."

"I thought I might become a forest ranger."

He was sober and impenetrable, as at the first moment they met. Caroline felt sorry for his parents. "We thought we'd look for an apartment in Boston. I come from around there," she explained. "I'm going back to graduate school to finish my degree, and I might have a job as a teaching assistant at the same time. Ivan . . . isn't quite sure yet what he'll do. But there are a lot of opportunities in his field up there. I'm sure it won't be difficult."

Ivan sat back with his arms folded, studying her.

"Thank you, Caroline," his mother said pointedly. "That sounds reasonable. We were just interested. After all."

"Congratulations. You've become a wife," said Ivan.

Soon it was time to go.

"But don't you kids want to stay overnight? I made up the bed in the guest room. Or if that isn't big enough for you, this couch right here opens into a double bed."

"Mom, I told you we were staying in the city."

"Yes, but I thought if you stayed late you might want to . . ."

"We can still catch the last train back."

"You're sure, now? Don't worry, we'll let you sleep as late as you want in the morning."

"Thanks, but it's all arranged. Caroline never stayed in a hotel in New York. We thought it would be . . . kind of a treat."

"Oh, of course. I see. Well, remember, you can stay here anytime till you get settled. A hotel can run into money."

"Thanks anyway, Mom." He kissed his mother good-bye.

Ivan's father drove them to the station. They were just in time. In the train Caroline took off her shoes, leaned her head back and sighed.

"I guess they can be pretty hard to take," he said.

"Not at all. I liked them. They were awfully nice to me. I'm just not used to it. Ivan, do you think we'll ever get back to Rome?"

"Oh, sometime, I guess. Maybe in our wheelchairs."

She laughed. "I can just see that. I'll wheel you around St. Peter's."

"But who will wheel you?"

"I will be self-propelled."

He stroked her hair. "You look tired. Well, we won't be seeing them very often."

"What a way to talk about your own parents. My parents wouldn't have been so friendly to a total stranger. You don't appreciate them. What have you got against them?"

"Nothing, really. Only that they make me feel about twelve years old." He put his hand on her leg.

"Well, if that's how you behave . . ."

"Don't. I have a mother already." He leaned into the aisle and peered through the car, which was empty except for two solitary men up front. He moved his hand up under her skirt.

"Ivan! Here?"

"Shh."

They did what Caroline told Ivan's parents they would do. Their apartment was in an old section of Boston known for its appeal to young couples of modest incomes and enthusiasms for the finer things. The building stood on a broad street shrouded by maples and lined with brownstones whose complex filigrees were blurring with age. To Caroline nothing was more sturdily comforting than their wide street and its forthright, settling houses, but Ivan, expert in such matters, liked to remind her that it was built on landfill. Where they walked each day was not as solid as it felt; it had once been shifting river banks.

Back in the doctoral program she switched from statistics to geometric topology. In topology you pushed shapes around so that spaces within and without transformed into new spaces: a protean vocation. You could smooth out bumps and knot up curves and play with dimensions like a god, teasing and testing how far a configuration might be deformed yet still keep its fundamental nature and properties intact. Three mornings a week she taught introductory calculus to freshmen. Ivan got a job doing research in architectural history for the Institute for Studies in the Humanities, a nonprofit organization of vague ameliorative purpose and connections to the nearby universities. Besides that, he was working on a book about the relation of Rome's architecture to its history. When they unpacked, Caroline found he had piles of notes on his meanderings and readings, even several chapters already outlined.

"I thought you loafed the whole time."

"I never said that." At home, among his overflowing cartons, his books by visionaries like Lewis Mumford and Buckminster Fuller, Ivan seemed distinctly exotic. He wore dungarees and blue work shirts around the house like the young husbands in apartments above and below, but his hair was long and his expression lacked their frank, or blank, simplicity. So she did marry someone exotic after all. She smiled to herself. When her mother had worried over her lack of interest in the upstanding boys in town, she used to threaten to marry an African, or an Arab.

"When did you do all this?" She pointed to the ragged notebooks. "Before you met me, I suppose."

"Most of it. We didn't meet till June, remember? But I did some after too. Nights."

"Certainly not toward the end?"

"No, I guess not."

"I must have interfered with your project."

"It doesn't matter. You were an interesting project too."

It pleased her to find he was a serious worker, like a surprise icing on a cake, but it hardly mattered. For she had accepted him, serious or idle; was not marriage the unconditional acceptance?

As Ivan had wished, they shared the pots and pans and the food in them, and he no longer had to carry his hairbrush around late at night. They shopped and cooked together, and every few weeks spent a Saturday afternoon cleaning up the apartment's accumulated mess while Caroline's records spun for hours on the phonograph. Afterwards, so as not to dirty their pristine kitchen, they would bring in pizza or Chinese food, then make love in slow, passive exhaustion on clean sheets and allow a new mess to begin accumulating.

They made friends with neighbors, and with people from the math department and from Ivan's Institute, along with their husbands and wives. Male and female created he them, and male and female the serious young hordes set forth in tandem, as if every movie or party or picnic were as charged with perilous mission as Noah's journey in the Ark. The era of togetherness blazed in its fading years with the luminosity of decadence. Caroline and Ivan were preeminent among couples striving to create a dyad of unshakable firmness, with a near-perfect meshing of parts. They did not even need to try too hard. As discordant as their courtship had been, so harmonious was their marriage. They had taken the vows.

"You two are disgusting," one woman said. "You even talk to each other at parties." They chalked it up to envy.

She loved the cold winters. She wanted Ivan to skate with her on the pond in the Public Garden, after work, in the bluish dusk of January, but he found excuses. Not long ago she had been ready to face two months alone in Italy; now she found she could not skate alone less than half a mile from home.

"Come on, please. It would be so nice. You can leave your book for a while."

"I just don't feel like it today."

"Don't you remember, when you were a kid, how great it felt—you get all warm, and the stars come out? We used to have a pond in town. We went after school and stayed till suppertime. We skated so long that walking felt funny after."

"There aren't a lot of ponds around Fourteenth Street."

They were getting dressed for work. Ivan was scrutinizing his ties. He hated to wear a tie but owned dozens: he liked them as abstract designs.

She came over and reached her arms around his neck. "Can I ask you a personal question?"

He grunted.

"Do you know how to skate?"

He pulled her close to him. She could feel his head shaking from side to side.

"Did you ever skate?"

He nodded.

"Aha, you fell, right?"

"It's a ridiculous means of locomotion."

"Listen, and look at me. Meet me tonight, around six, when there's hardly anyone left, and I will teach you how to skate."

Shivering in the dark, she sat down on a bench to wait. The only others on the pond were two small girls of about eight, with an older girl in charge. Good; little girls would not shame him. He was habitually late, she was discovering. It was a mode of protest, like a nervous tic. When he finally arrived he put on the skates in silence and leaned on her like a cripple. She led him from the snow-covered ground to the ice feeling like a dedicated nurse in the physical therapy room of a hospital. With her arm around his waist his body sagged into its own gravity. They stood still for a moment in the crisp darkness with the trees looming, strange bulbous shapes. In the anonymous dark it could be any winter: he could be eighty, not thirty, and she seventy-five. He was a heavy, ancient shell of a man, but her burden, and she would be loyal to the end, holding him until he made the trip into darkness on his own. It was not a vision of horror, only of bleakness, and doubly vivid because so entwined were their imaginations that she suspected Ivan was seeing the same thing. A *folie à deux,* the most pernicious kind.

He nudged her. "Well, let's get moving," he said gruffly.

"Okay! First just try to walk. Pick your feet up."

After a number of turns on her arm he was ready to try it alone. And after a few tentative turns by himself he began to glide and to skim a bit. His body lost its hunched tension as he glided to and fro like some young night bird practicing easy swoops. He crashed into Caroline in order to stop— he didn't know yet how to stop himself. Every time she saw him veering proudly in her direction she steeled her muscles to bear the weight thudding into her. Ivan found this crashing and her patient stiffness tremendously funny, and clowning in an antic way, crashed far more often than necessary. He was delighted with himself, and planning on figure eights for next time. Hallelujah, he could skate, she thought as she watched him disappear round the bend of the center island. He would be a good skater, and he would skate alone. He was out of sight, skating somewhere off and on his own, and she felt a profound, guilty relief.

They made the desired advances. Caroline finished her Ph.D. and became an instructor, which meant more courses to teach and more money. More respect, too, than she had anticipated, being one of the few women in a man's field, and even a small reputation for her research, she noticed when she attended conferences. Still fewer women ventured into the esoteric theory of knots. The older professors, especially, looked at her askance, but in the end had to offer a grudging approval. She undertook a new project in elementary transcendental functions, and also supervised graduate students, whom Ivan liked to refer to as her boys. When she came home drained and fell into a chair after four hours of conferences, he would bring her a Scotch and say, "What's the matter? The boys give you a rough time?" Besides working at the Institute, Ivan published two chapters of his book in architectural magazines and was asked to serve on the Mayor's Advisory Council for historic preservation. He wrote occasional articles for *The Nation*. He might have taught at one of the universities had he wished to, but he thought that would be taking on too much.

At each of these advances, after the celebrating, Caroline was left with a hollow, vertiginous feeling, as though someone had punched her lightly in the stomach. Happenings were spinning and spinning in a widening orbit of which she was the center. It dizzied her to watch them spin, yet she seemed to possess the stasis of a still center. She could not trace how she had gotten to that point. How she had become that point. Somewhere along the way she had relinquished something—motion, life. The more that happened, the more inert she felt.

Ivan's mother asked a funny question when she telephoned every week. She asked, "Are you making each other happy?" Had she not known Ivan's decorous mother, Caroline might have found it intrusively intimate. But Ivan's mother was not referring to sex. Depending on her mood, Caroline smiled or frowned, but always said politely, "Yes, of course." Ivan never answered it directly. If he was in good spirits he teased and said, "Tell me what happy is and I'll tell you if we're making each other it." But if he was feeling sullen, as he often was these days, from overwork, he said, exasperated, "Mom, really!"

"What does she literally mean by that?" Caroline asked him one night after they hung up.

"God only knows," he said, pouring a drink.

"Are married people required to make each other happy? Besides everything else?"

"I wouldn't know," said Ivan. "It sounds like too great a burden to me."

Many evenings they spent together in the extra room they had fixed up as a study, with the desks against facing walls so that they worked with their backs to each other. She liked to imagine that although their heads were bent in opposite directions on separate endeavors, a current of warmth and connection pulsed between them. One night she raised her head and felt nothing, the absence of the current. A current needed to be fueled: the fuel was depleted, sucked away, she didn't know how. She turned. Ivan's head was bent over and he was writing. He did not feel her stare. She walked around the room.

"Do you want to stop and have some coffee?" she asked.

After a long while he answered, "No," without looking up.

That was all right; she understood what it was to be absorbed. Later he would seek her out, in bed. There he was absorbed in her. The air in the room became suddenly thick and stifling. She opened the window wide. Ivan's papers fluttered and rattled.

"Could you lower that a little, please?" he said without looking up.

She shut the window and fled to the bedroom. Waiting in bed, she read back issues of *The Nation*, mostly articles Ivan had written, because she enjoyed his style, which was epigrammatic yet fluid and complex. He analyzed the social causes of the deterioration of urban spaces with an unyielding lucidity not always displayed when he spoke. The lucidity reminded her of the novels of Jane Austen, favorites of her youth, and she recalled unhappily how, in them, all action comes to an abrupt end with marriage. Satisfying as

Jane Austen was, Caroline used to sit up wondering, at the last page, what happened then, and then, and after that? What would happen to her, now, that could move her? Anything? Irritated, she began smoking, though Ivan hated the smell hanging over the bed. Hers were foolish, childish complaints. The trouble was only in her expectations. Her naïveté. The trouble was only that before, she had looked forward to a future of large and unimaginable changes, twists and turns, and now the future was mundanely imaginable and linear: professional advancement, a larger apartment, vacations. A reasonably good time. She took off her plain wedding ring and revolved it between her fingers. Was it only a trick of language that in topology the circle is called a trivial knot? When Ivan came to bed she greeted him with a savage passion, but it was partly sham. She was restless. She wanted it, not him.

Their connection was fading, losing its vibrancy, as a print hanging on the wall too long loses the vigor of its colors, and indeed the prints he had brought back from Italy, of splendid old buildings and terraced countryside, were losing their color, hanging for several years in the unrelenting sunlight of the east windows. Caroline understood now what their friend had meant about their being disgusting: at parties they circulated. They talked to other people, they flirted. Dancing with some man, she drifted off into a dark corner in a tight erotic embrace. It was interesting, he had an interesting body. Different from Ivan's. Of course Ivan, with his contacts, would take in everything. She and the man unlocked; fifteen minutes later she saw Ivan kissing his wife. That was all right too. They were even. It would never be mentioned, except maybe months from now, as a joke.

They went to the movies a lot, but she liked films about love and family bonds, films of desire and strife, betrayal and sacrifice, while he liked films about politics—struggle and power, strategy and intrigue. They sat through each other's films patiently, but Ivan usually found Caroline's favorites to be oversimplifications, with earnest good people aligned against devious bad people. In his favorites she found good and evil washed together in a spreading amoral gray, and she argued that such a high degree of ambiguity destroyed all distinctions. Life was like that, he replied; things were not as distinct as they had been taught in school. She could forgive a good deal of grossness so long as there was not emotional dishonesty, but he required aesthetic purity and was harsh about lapses in taste. He said that if something was shoddily executed it had unquestionably been shoddily conceived and insufficiently felt. This rigor in him, especially when directed at a well-meaning movie, gave her a sinking, hopeless feeling. Yet she knew that it was so in her own work: everything true and useful proceeded from a clear statement of the premises.

They agreed that power corrupts, but Caroline believed it corrupted so absolutely that there was no hope of improvement through sanctioned channels. The problem, as she sketched it out for Ivan one afternoon in the park, began with the social contract, when more than three or four people gathered together and made rules. Then they felt important and set about policing the observance of their rules, and from this feeling of importance flowed all social ills. It was very simple. It could happen even to good people, with good rules. So, she was an anarchist, she told Ivan, but added laughingly that he must not tell anyone at the university or she would lose her job. Of course she would not throw a bomb into an occupied building, but in her heart she was an anarchist. Ivan thought this sequence of logic was ineffectual. Perhaps he thought it was funny too, but he did not laugh at her opinions—he was unfailingly respectful and courteous. What good is a closet anarchist, he asked courteously, pulling petals from a daisy. If she really believed as she said, she should take the shuttle down to New York and bomb the stock exchange. She said he was not being fair. Anarchism was far more than throwing bombs and he knew it; he knew she was referring to freedom from superimposed social restrictions, freedom to become. That was all very well, said Ivan, everyone wanted freedom. Ah yes, personal freedom. Especially those members of the more privileged classes wanted it, who had never known the lack of money. And he gave her a curiously detached look. However, if she had any practical commitment she should do as he suggested, bomb the stock exchange; even though his father had finally acquired some small holdings, he would testify on her behalf. But she should do it at night, when no one would get hurt. For his part, he preferred to make small, incremental but tangible improvements through the existing system. You could never dismantle the entire corporate structure, so you might as well do what you could in your own small way. In either case you were not going to get very far. Therefore he loved enduring beauty, and chose to spend weekend afternoons looking at paintings in galleries and museums. Well then, she wanted to know, if he felt that way about incremental change and enduring beauty, why did he subscribe to the *National Guardian,* whose self-righteous, unbeautiful hysteria made her laugh? Because they had something to say, he replied, tearing another daisy, and it was important to hear all sides, particularly those the popular press ignored. She had no answer for that, but she muttered that she didn't relish being referred to as a member of the privileged classes merely because her father had been a high school teacher, and moreover, she had no intention of apologizing for being born too late to appreciate the Depression.

But months later, walking on the wet sand of the beach

on Cape Cod, where they rented a summer place for three weeks, each one confessed, in a rare moment of closeness, that they believed the other more intelligent. They were mutually surprised, after all the thrust and counterthrust of debate, and demurred with embarrassed modesty, then clasped hands and continued on, with the mild surf lapping at their feet. The only disparity, thought Caroline, was that her compliment to him was tinged with candid admiration, and his to her with shadowy resentment.

"Well, you're prettier, anyway," Ivan said. "At least we can agree on that."

"Oh, I don't know," she teased. "I'm not so sure."

She looked at him, tanned and rested, still younger than his thirty-three years, and he did appear beautiful. She embraced him and urged him to a nook of the beach behind some rocks, for though they still made love all the time and with a new restless energy, it was seldom that they could make love with a fullness of heart, as they used to.

In her spare time Caroline read novels and poetry, while Ivan read books about social issues or the history of art. If he read a novel it was something she had never heard of, like *Elective Affinities,* or *The Last Puritan,* or *The Man Without Qualities,* novels which, she found on leafing through them, treated reality in a large and unsparing way that made her uneasy. The titles themselves, alluding to life's absences, intimidated her. Because Ivan himself, who picked those books, seemed absent. Present to the touch but absent to the more discerning senses. His desire for her had become a conundrum. Why had he wanted her to be always with him, if he was absent himself?

While she felt herself and Ivan fading away from each other, receding like figures in a thick fog, she read book after book by Henry James. They were the perfect mental nourishment: pungent but safely digestible. Everyone renounced what they wanted most, and never had to face the worse pain of getting what they wanted most. Sometimes she worried that Ivan, with his books about issues and his brilliant but neglected novels, was getting an ever firmer grip on reality, while she, with her daily forays into the equivalences of non-trivial knots as well as into Henry James and his more fey contemporaries, was losing hers. But perhaps they did not both need such a firm grip on reality. Perhaps Ivan could do that for her. The principle of any organization was a suitable division of labor. Lately, in fact, with both of them so busily engrossed in work foreign to the other, it had seemed wasteful to cook together and clean up together, so they had devised a system of alternate nights. It was lonesome in the kitchen, but more efficient.

There was a woman at his office, he told her one night at dinner, who did the same kind of research as he did. They were working on a project together, a plan to take museum holdings out on loan in city vehicles so that people in poor neighborhoods who didn't go to museums could see beautiful things. Of course, the security problems were overwhelming—the project might never get off the ground. This woman had an unusual name, Chantal. She also had an unusual life. Her father had been in the diplomatic corps, so she spent her childhood in foreign parts, and went to the Sorbonne. She was about forty, Ivan would guess, and had no children. She was married to a painter named Joe who lived in New York. One week out of every month Joe came up to Boston to stay with Chantal in her rehabilitated brownstone.

"And that's how they're married?" said Caroline.

"Yes."

"That's kind of odd. I mean, do they want to be together or not?"

"I suppose they want to be together for one week a month.

He's involved in something down there, a cooperative gallery or something, and anyhow, he likes it. She prefers it here."

"How convenient. I suppose she has . . . other men, for the three weeks that Joe is not around?"

Ivan gave her his sideways critical look and shrugged. "I don't know anything about that part of her life. She's very nice, though. Very interesting. I thought maybe we might have her over for dinner one night."

"Hm," said Caroline, taking more spaghetti. Ivan had cooked tonight, superbly. Spaghetti al pesto, green and grainy. His best efforts were in foreign, exotic dishes. He could cook the night Chantal came over too. Caroline did not plan to like her. It seemed unjust that Chantal should have the advantages of both the married and the single states. She knew already what this Chantal would look like: she would wear long dark flowered skirts and long earrings and have dark eyes and long dark hair. Everything about her would be long and dark and rather droopy, but she would have broad shoulders and broad hips. She would look like an elegant peasant.

Chantal did not come over for dinner, since Ivan did not suggest inviting her again. Her name came up when he talked about the Artmobile, and once in a while he mentioned having lunch with her, either with a group of people or alone. He became even busier at work and had to stay late nights at the office once or twice a week. Not for the Artmobile, he said; it was something else—the architectural competition for the new city hall. On one of those late nights Caroline lay in bed reading *The Golden Bowl*. The name of the character who came between the young couple in the novel was Charlotte, and when she saw this name on the page she thought of Chantal. She raised her eyes from the book. The tableau before her—dresser with comb, brush and bottles of perfume, strands of beads hanging from nails in the wall, bookshelves, print of Degas dancers bending over stiffly to tie their shoes—was suddenly unfamiliar. She was a stranger in her own bedroom. Right at this moment Ivan might be screwing Chantal. Maybe Chantal was moaning with pleasure. Or screaming—maybe she was the type who screamed. Or no, maybe she was having a hard time getting there. Oh yes, she liked that notion very much, Chantal straining fruitlessly for an orgasm, under Ivan. Maybe she never came at all. But then Ivan wouldn't be sprawled on top of her—Ivan required a response. Some men's self-esteem resided in having an erection, but Ivan's, conveniently, resided in eliciting a response. It might be his first time with Chantal, though. He would soon catch on and never go back, unless he thought she was worth saving from such perdition. No, Ivan hadn't the soul of a missionary. Maybe he was having trouble himself. Maybe Chantal was coaxing it along. Probably not; that was not his sort of trouble. Still and all, a new person, the secrecy, the guilt. Even so stalwart a man as Ivan . . .

She realized in shame that all her fantasies were of crude mechanical failure. But in all probability it was nothing like that. Ivan was magnetic and irresistible, Chantal was a dark, passionate gypsy. She put aside her book, and closing her eyes to the alien room, acknowledged hollowly that despite the vivid pictures in her mind, she was feeling nothing.

That was horrible, to feel nothing. Neither revulsion nor jealousy nor desire, only irritation, as if some stranger had borrowed an essential household article and would surely return it in a deteriorated condition. Was this what her promising life had become, sitting up alone in bed while her husband was off fucking a woman of eccentric habits, and feeling nothing except a niggardly irritation? She tried to imagine what would make Ivan go to this woman: loneliness, boredom, restlessness. They were what she felt too, except her mind would not fix on any of them—they formed a turgid medium she had moved into so insensibly and drifted in for so long. What she could readily imagine, and with a small stirring of tenderness, was how he would approach Chantal: his diffidence, the pained longing and dread he had had when first approaching her. What drew him? Her name, first of all. A romantic name, Chantal, he would love to say it. She could share his pleasure in the beauty of the sound. He would use the special tone of voice to say, "Chantal," the tone he used when he was moved by love and desire, and which she heard less and less of late. And then, his touch on Chantal. Her skin, her hair. She was feeling for Ivan, who was so close to her, after all, feeling for Ivan's pleasure in the touch. Let him have that wonder with Chantal, if he no longer had it with her. Everyone should have that. She thought of the ways he made love, of gestures and caresses of his that had grown into being on her body, shaped and tailored to envelop her like a second skin, and returned in kind, so that in the dark they still found a sustaining presence, despite the absence so visible in the light of day. But what if these ways did not fit so well on Chantal? Chantal was a different body; maybe she needed a different sort of lover. Past all sense, she wished that Ivan should please Chantal, for the sake of his pride, so that the lover that he was would be truly recognized. For the sake of her own pride as well, for the lover that he was, was hers. And at last she was with them, neuter and unaroused, but partaking of his giving and of her receiving, that it should go well.

Ivan came in. She pretended to be asleep. He undressed quietly, came into bed and put his arms around her.

"Are you asleep?" he whispered.

She didn't answer.

"Caroline," he persisted. "Are you awake?"

"I'm not sure."

"Be awake, Caroline."

"Why?"

"Why do you think?"

She had already extended herself, in fantasy, beyond her powers. This was asking too much.

"Aren't you tired?" she said.

"Not too tired. Come on. Come to me."

She did not want to touch him because of the possibility of Chantal, but she wanted him to touch her. Exhausted and empty, she wanted to do nothing, only to receive love. Ivan understood, and she in turn gave him the response he sought. And because for the life of her she could not tell whether he sought her after a solitary evening working, or after Chantal, who disappointed or aroused him beyond measure, she wept.

"What's the matter, baby? Wasn't it good for you?"

"Yes, yes. It's . . . Ivan, I have this awful feeling . . . something is very wrong between us, and I can't bear it."

He was quiet. She expected that he would brush it off or else had fallen asleep.

"I know. I know. But I am just so exhausted I can't talk about anything now. Can we talk about it another time?"

On the way home from work a few weeks later she stopped in a bookstore to buy a birthday present for Lila, the five-year-old daughter of friends who lived downstairs. Lila was a precocious, wispy child who was already learning to read. Lately she would ring their doorbell weekends and, clutching a book to her chest, step shyly over the threshold. Ivan held her on his knee and read whatever she had brought with her, and then in a deep dramatic voice told her stories of fairies and ogres and elves. Lila took them to be real, and he did not disillusion her.

Caroline had never been in the children's section before. Quickly seduced, she read book after book straight through, and left an hour later feeling exalted, as though she had traveled to far-off places. There was an entire subculture, complete with a literature that embodied the consciousness of its race—children—as thoroughly as any literature did for its people. Springing with life, it was an alternative more appealing than the corrupted mainstream. To inhabit it, though, you needed either to be a child or to have a child.

"Look what I bought for Lila," she said that evening. Ivan was lying on the couch reading, one hand under his head and one hand holding the book upright on his chest, the way her father used to do after dinner.

"Let me see," he said. "Ah. *When We Were Very Young.* I don't think she has that."

"I think you'll like it. Do you know, when I browsed through all those children's books in the store I had an epiphany."

"Really? You mean like James Joyce?"

"I think I would like to have a baby."

"A baby."

"Yes. It's easy to do. You just do what we do all the time, except without—"

"Will you please stop talking like an idiot?" Ivan sat up and put *The Tale of Genji* aside. "You want to have a baby. I'm a little surprised. The other day you said, and I quote, conjugal life was overrated."

"I know. But I changed my mind. This would be something productive."

"People who have babies to . . . to prop up marriages—that is the worst thing in the world."

"Yes, yes, I know. But it's not for that. We're not in

such bad shape, really. I mean, look, we can still make love. People on the verge of . . . of, you know . . . don't make love like we do."

"How do you know? That's a very naïve assumption. Anyway, sex means nothing. You can have sex with anybody."

She looked at him sharply but her voice was calm. "Oh. I don't know anything about that. I didn't think it meant nothing."

"Well, not nothing. But the point is . . ." He scrutinized her with doubt. "You're sure you want to have a baby?"

"Why, you like Lila, don't you? You like children."

"Lila visits. Our own would live here. But that's not an answer."

"No, I'm not sure. I only thought it might be interesting. I'm waiting to hear your opinion."

"Caroline!"

"What?"

"Why are you talking like this?"

"Like what?"

"You know what I mean. You don't sound like yourself."

"Because I don't know how to talk to you any more," she cried. "I don't know where you are and what you're becoming. You don't tell me anything. The only time we make any contact is in bed. What the hell is this all about?"

Ivan bent over with his head in his hands. When he sat up again his face was washed over with gray. "That's not true."

"Almost true."

He took her hand in both of his. His hands were warm and large, and her hand disappeared between them. He placed her hand on his thigh.

"Oh, that's a lot easier than talking, Ivan, sure. But it doesn't change anything."

He let her hand go. "You don't even want me for that any more. What do you want me for, then? To help you make a baby?"

There were tears in his eyes. Caroline's heart flipped over. Her inner organs shriveled up, and for a moment she feared her shriveled heart would stop beating altogether. But she wouldn't touch him. She said, "You think that's your best feature? You're mistaken."

"I think you've had it with me. I knew this would happen." Ivan leaned back and stretched both arms across the back of the couch: he was spread out like an offering. If she wasn't careful she would be climbing on him to ease her frustration, but it would not be eased, just stifled.

"No. I can stick anything out. I've waited out death twice. It's you. You don't love me any more," she said. "You only love yourself. Your projects. Your work. Your pleasures."

"I do love you," he said bitterly. The words sounded squeezed out of him, as in an interrogation. Caroline's eyes widened in pain. "All right, I didn't mean it like that, wait a minute," he said. He closed his eyes and rested his hands on his thighs, extending the long taut fingers. He breathed in and exhaled like an exhausted runner. "I do love you," he repeated quietly. "But you're sticking it out."

"You can be very perverse. I'll stick it out because I love you. Because it matters to me. But still, something is very wrong."

"Nothing out of the ordinary. This is what real life is like. It gets to be . . . inert."

"I'll never accept that," she said. "If that's so, then I don't want to be ordinary."

"What, then?"

"It would not be inert if we were available to each other."

"Available to each other! I hate that kind of jargon."

"All right. Be a purist. But you are somewhere else, Ivan."

"Tell me where I am then, Caroline."

"I wish I knew. Maybe . . . maybe with Chantal."

He stood up and walked to the window. "Don't be ridiculous. I thought you were going to say something profound. Metaphysical. An epiphany!"

"Not that I care," she said. "Not that I care. It's just that if you are, she certainly takes it out of you."

He whirled around. "Shut up about that! Do you know what you're doing to me when you say that? How can you say such things?" He flung himself into a chair and flung himself up again. He paced. "You're venomous, you know? You're crude. You're like an ax. You're killing me."

She was amazed at how hard she had suddenly become. Her body received this as if she were a stone. "Ivan," she answered coolly, "I can't even get near enough to kill you."

"And you want a baby. To bring a baby into this."

"Yes. I know this is very ugly, right now. But it's not the whole thing. It's a . . . *brutto periodo.*"

"A what?"

"Don't you remember? A *brutto periodo.* It has to pass."

"Oh, her." Ivan sat down on the couch again. "That seems like another century. Look, Caroline, this is obviously not getting us anywhere. I don't need scenes like this. We'd be better off living separately."

"We would not. Look at everyone scrambling around and switching partners, like a square dance. Do you honestly want that? You're not going to find anyone who would understand you better than I do. And I'd probably never find anyone who would put up with me."

"But don't you see, this kind of understanding is . . . is lethal. I can do without it," said Ivan. His voice softened, though. It gave up the hard, sealed edge. "If you understand so much, understand that I can't be something I'm not."

"That's not what I'm asking. I'm asking you to be what you are. Were."

"Then tell me exactly what you want from me that you don't have."

She shook her head. "I don't know what else to call it."

"Caroline, let's stop this. I want some peace."

"I don't like peace. I mean, that sort of peace. It's easy to be at peace when two people don't want anything from each other, but just occupy the same space. That's not peace, that's a vacuum."

Ivan closed his eyes.

After a long silence she said, "Barbara and Rick got their divorce papers yesterday. I met her on campus. She looked terrible. And Christine is having an affair with an actor in her company and is miserable about it. Cory and Joan are separating. I got a letter from her today."

"Cory and Joan?"

"Yes. She didn't say exactly how it came about. But for one thing he's drinking an awful lot and she can't live with that. It scares the baby too."

"Cory drinking?" Ivan gave her a puzzled frown. "Cory was like a child."

"Yes. But people grow up, you know. I don't want to be like that. I don't want to see you like that."

"That's awful. Cory." He got up and paced the room again. "I don't get it. They all seemed happy enough to me."

"Oh, happy." She waved an arm in dismissal.

"What's wrong with happy?"

Caroline laughed briefly. "Don't you remember, you were the one who said happiness is not the point."

"Did I? What did I say the point was?"

"You didn't say. I'm not surprised at all those breakups. I could tell. There were things . . ."

"Well, I don't delve the way you do," said Ivan, sitting down beside her again.

Caroline shifted sideways to face him. She touched his arm lightly. "Ivan. Let's not be like that. Let's be different. We'll last."

"I'm sure they all felt that way."

"You wanted me to marry you," she said softly, "so that I would always be here. So I did. I am here, and I will always be here. Now I want something, Ivan. I want to have a baby."

At last he turned around and looked her straight in the face. She saw that some barrier, at last, had yielded. He was fully present, as if they were joined in an embrace.

"Ah, you did change your mind," he said. "Did you get a feeling, right here, or here?" He knew by now exactly where everything was in a woman.

Her eyes filled. "No. To tell the truth. But simply because this . . . is not enough."

"You mean," he said, not moving his eyes from her face, "I'm not enough."

"No, not you," she protested. She felt, remotely, tears dripping off her lashes. "This is not enough."

"All right."

"But do you want it?"

"I said all right."

"That's not the same as wanting it."

"It'll have to do. You've gotten what you wanted, Caroline, haven't you? Take the claws out of me."

"I'm sorry. I am. But I'm not trying to win a victory. I'm saying it because, you know, you'll have to be a father. Will you do that?"

"Oh Jesus! Yes, I'll be a father. It's my kid too. What do you take me for?"

Caroline thought it would be so easy. Everyone else managed to do it in a flash, managed so well that half the women she knew had at some time taken the weekend economy flight to Puerto Rico for an abortion. She had scant pity now for those horror stories. What was wrong with her and Ivan! In algebra, if only you persevered, eventually you would get results. But in human endeavors there was no just correlation between effort and results. She and Ivan, like the aborters, were the proof. Her flat stomach was, anyway, as it was equally the envy of friends working on their second or third.

A few careless words, and soon advice and sympathy poured in from all quarters. Obvious cripples were treated with respect; they were patronized. A pair of freakish losers. Caroline did not care if the problem lay in him or her or both or neither; she was only vastly irritated. So was Ivan. The irritation spilled out onto the advice-giving friends, who maddeningly excused them—the strain they were under. They could not afford to be too irritated with each other. Anger, they already knew, could be a powerful aphrodisiac; irritation was not.

They did not try hard enough, it was suggested. There were ways open that their pride balked at. Caroline would not take her temperature for five minutes every morning and enter it on a chart, seizing the hottest occasions for sex and graphing the event. *Carpe diem,* Ivan called the chart. She called it Frequency of Fucking. She would rather die barren than divulge to a doctor the patterns of hers and

Ivan's desire, or lack of it. Yet the vulgar truth was that she needn't graph the frequency of desire, merely of performance. Once these were a single line, now split and diverged along separate paths. They desired without performing, performed without desiring.

She studied the chart as they sat drinking Scotch before dinner. Ivan leafed through the *National Guardian,* which had gone wild over the Cuban missile crisis. A past master at graphs, Caroline found this one a poor job. Messy. An uncontrolled experiment with a highly imperfect grasp of the complexity of factors involved. The data, because they were incomplete, might incorporate gross and misleading fluctuations, with no means of correction. Aesthetically, it offended—the sophomores under her guidance could do as well. But of course aesthetics was not her concern. Her concern was to get pregnant. You did that by placing a dot, placing an asterisk, placing a letter. There was a code, with a legend.

"Aha! I bet you don't need to record it if you do it orally," she remarked.

"What are you muttering about?" Ivan asked, still reading. "An oral thermometer?"

"Oral sex."

He coughed discreetly. "I would imagine not. What for?"

"Tut tut, I guess that's out, then. Unless I want to try growing it in my throat."

He gave her the sidelong look, a disapproving schoolteacher. She tossed the chart aside. "I don't have the patience for this stupid thing. I can't think about this first thing in the morning. I have to go to work."

Ivan turned pages. "It is incredible," he said, "how close we came to a full-scale nuclear war."

"Ivan. How would you like to beat the system by performing an indecent act?"

Always a selective listener, he put the *Guardian* down promptly. "I wouldn't mind."

And if she would not keep a chart, the other option was even more unthinkable. She knew Ivan. She knew exactly what he would and would not do for her. He would stay married and be a father, but he would not follow a white-coated attendant into a small room where Muzak played, and jerk off into a plastic container while studying photos in *Playboy, Hustler,* and *Swank.* She did not even bother to suggest it.

Ivan did not wilt from anxiety. He became more potent, with a raging determination to get the better of nature, which in its futility grieved her heart. She wished she could explain that this was not an experiment in physics, where increased thrust and depth and velocity might make a difference, but in chemistry, a more subtle, less easily controlled discipline. But she could not hurt him in that way; she had never been the sort to give critiques in bed, so she shut her eyes and suffered it. When he exploded within her she felt relief, and thought about probability theory. She forgot what it could be like without a goal.

Her own reaction to failure was nausea. There were sporadic stretches when she was barely able to eat, spells of vomiting bile from an empty stomach, headaches and dizziness. At the beginning she thought they were viral infections going around, but they came too often for that. They came when everyone else was feeling fine.

She hoped she would be all right for the Valentine's Day party given by one of Ivan's colleagues at the Institute. They arrived late, as usual; Ivan had to finish reading a proposal. As they entered they were each handed a small red satin heart to pin on. Ivan said, "Maybe I should wear my heart on my sleeve."

"You! You're hardly the type," she replied. "Wear your

heart on your heart, that's good enough."

Ivan wandered off and Caroline sat down near a friend, Antonia.

"There you are at last. I have Jerome for you," Antonia whispered, nodding at a plump man opposite, who was lighting a pipe. "Don't you have a drink?"

Antonia, a former ballet dancer, had recently given birth to twin boys. She came to these parties sullen and bedraggled, but as the night wore on her eyes began to sparkle: she drank the hours away and usually had to be carried home by her husband, who worked with Ivan.

"No, I'm not drinking tonight."

"Why not? Are you saving yourself for the pot later on?"

"No," said Caroline. "No pot either. I just don't feel like it. Hi, Jerome. Hi, Sheila."

After a seemingly endless period of psychiatric training and analysis, Jerome was starting a practice. Because he was a zealot, Caroline badgered him as a matter of principle. Sheila, his wife, was in the final stages of pregnancy.

"What's the matter, are you queasy again?" asked Sheila. Her hands were clasped around her stomach as if it might detach and roll away.

"Oh, just a little. So, Jerome, how is business? Have you encountered anything like the Wolf Man yet? Or Dora, poor girl? Remember you told me about Freud and Dora?"

He held the pipe between his teeth. He wore his satin heart on the knot of his striped tie, over his throat. "Your symptoms sound like morning sickness." Perhaps to keep the pipe in place, he barely moved his lips when he spoke.

"Hardly that."

"You sure?" asked Sheila.

"I'm sure. But really, Jerome, how's it going? Are there enough willing neurotics in the Boston-Cambridge area? I imagine this would be a fertile field."

Antonia put a restraining hand on her arm. "Caroline," she whispered, "don't be outrageous. Jerome's not in a good mood."

"What happened," she whispered back, "faulty transference?"

"My diagnosis is, just horny."

"It's coming along," said Jerome. "Fortunately, most people are not quite as resistant to their own best interests as you are."

"Aha! Now what is that supposed to mean?" She lit a cigarette, even though smoking sometimes made her sick.

"I've told you before, for your problem you ought to seek help. Then you'd be able to drink at parties, at least." Jerome removed the pipe, and taking from his lapel pocket a small tubular chrome instrument with a sharp point, began cleaning it. He dug the instrument with mincing thrusts around the circumference of the bowl and dumped wads of tobacco into an ashtray. "Tell me something, just out of curiosity. When you were a little girl, how did you think babies were made?"

"I believed in the Immaculate Conception," said Antonia. "I always wanted to do it that way. I think that's still one of my wish-fulfillment fantasies."

"That's another story. I'm asking Caroline."

"Oh, Jerome, take a night off."

He pointed the stem of the pipe at her. "What are you afraid of? I'm only making conversation."

"I don't remember. I think I always knew how it was done. I had a couple of rabbits for a while, in the backyard."

"Did it have any connection in your mind with eating and digestion?"

"Eating?"

"There is a common fantasy among girl children that a baby gets started because of something eaten. It's quite natu-

ral, because they see how it expands in the stomach region."
He cast a brief glance at his wife's stomach. "Like Sheila
here, a child might think she had eaten a watermelon
whole."

A wave of nausea rose through Caroline, and her thighs
felt watery. "I would eat, then, wouldn't I, to make it happen?"

Jerome leaned forward and tapped at her knee with the
empty bowl of his pipe. A few grains of tobacco fell to
her skirt. She stared at the little cluster they formed, a nearly
perfect hexagon. "It's not that simple," he said. "What
you're doing is rejecting food. You're fighting the idea of
pregnancy, obviously."

She put her hand to her throat. He was so close she could
see the pores around his nose. He smelled of pipe tobacco.
"That is the most ridiculous thing I ever heard."

She blinked several times. At the peripheries of her vision,
about Jerome's round face, shadowy scallops jiggled. The
room swayed and slowly turned. She leaned back. "He is
literally making me sick," she said to Antonia.

"Go lie down then, Caroline. You're a delicate shade
of green."

"Could she be unconsciously imitating the symptoms of
pregnancy, Jerome?" asked Sheila.

"Sheila, please," said Jerome with a cautionary look. He
replaced his pipe between his teeth, unlit, and tapped Caroline's knee with his fingers. He rested them there for a
moment. "Also, little girls are confused about how a baby
comes out. As an extension of the digestive metaphor, they
think—"

She rose, gripping the arm of the couch. "You know
you're quite a wit? That theory is second only to penis envy."
She looked around vaguely for Ivan, but Ivan was standing
way across the room, talking to some woman. "Pardon me

while I go throw up. Jerome, I think you have just violated the Hippocratic oath."

After she threw up she lay face down on the tile floor till her strength returned. She was used to it now; this was a short spasm. Once she washed her face and combed her hair she would look none the worse. Back in the party, she glimpsed Jerome leaning against the banister talking to another woman, a younger one, who was listening intently as he gestured toward her breasts with his pipe, from which a thin trail of smoke curled upward like a small tornado. Famished, Caroline ate half a roast beef sandwich and went off to find Ivan. On the way she tapped Jerome's companion on the shoulder. "I would watch out if I were you," she told her.

Ivan too was talking earnestly to an unknown blond woman, but he waved no object at her. They laughed together easily, like old friends. As Caroline approached he turned to make room for her in their tight space. He put his arm around her. "Caroline," he said, smiling, "I'd like you to meet Chantal Morgan. Chantal, my wife, Caroline."

"Hi." Chantal held out her hand. "Ivan talks a lot about you."

"Hello. I feel as though we should have met before," said Caroline, also smiling. Chantal! She had nearly forgotten about her over the past months. She looked neither frigid nor gypsy-like. She was slender and of medium height, with short shaggy hair and a blue dress that was short too, simple and almost severe. She wore no jewelry or make-up. Her face was very beautiful in an unproclaiming, sculptured way. When she laughed her light brown eyes narrowed, her severity disappeared, and she looked at Ivan and Caroline as though to draw them into her mirth. She was talking about how well Ivan had handled a crisis that arose with the Artmobile. One of the pieces had gotten slightly damaged while out on loan, and the museum director wanted to use that as an excuse to halt the project, but Ivan had managed to have the damage repaired and to placate the director. Caroline tried to imagine her flat on her back with her legs spread out for Ivan, but for once her imagination failed her.

"If it had been up to me, I would have argued and alienated him," Chantal said, "but Ivan is so diplomatic—he can get around anyone."

"Yes," said Caroline. She had never thought of him in quite that way, but now that Chantal pointed it out, she saw it was true.

"Is Joe in town?" asked Ivan.

"Yes, but he wouldn't come to this. He hates these kinds of parties." She laughed. "I left him in front of the TV with *The Man from U.N.C.L.E.*"

Toward the end of the party Ivan sat down on the floor in a small circle of people. They passed joints from mouth to mouth, from Antonia's mouth to Jerome's to Chantal's to Ivan's. He was high, ambling around in slow motion, touching the arms of women, with a dreamy smile. Caroline drove the car home through the falling snow and he lay back in the seat next to her, sighing from time to time.

"So that's Chantal," she said.

"Hm."

"She's not the way I pictured her."

"Hm?"

"She looks something like me, doesn't she? I mean, the same type."

"Mm-hm."

"Jerome says my nausea is a symptom of secretly not wanting to be pregnant. Subconsciously I think that if I keep the food down I'll get pregnant. Some hangover from childhood."

"Jerome is an asshole. If you provoke him, what do you expect?"

"I don't want to try to have a baby any more. I don't want to go to any more of these parties. I don't like any of our friends."

He gave a long sigh.

"Did you hear what I said?"

"I'm not deaf, Caroline. Deafness, unlike possible sterility, is not one of my infirmities," he intoned very slowly. "I hear everything you say. I hear every word, every syllable, every phoneme, every letter. I could repeat everything you have said in this car since we entered it. I am one of those people on whom, to quote one of your favorite authors, nothing is lost. In fact, at this very moment I hear music, I hear bells, and I hear that you don't want to have a baby, or go to any more of these parties, and you don't like any of our friends. Every . . . single . . . syllable."

At the next red light she turned and took a long look at him. "How much of that stuff did you smoke?" she said.

They were tired of Boston. The Back Bay, with its ever younger inhabitants, had grown too chic for their tastes. Their friends were defecting to the suburbs, where their preoccupations were formulas, night feedings and car seats, adultery, money, and analysis. When they visited, and Caroline saw and smelled the babies, watched the puréed foods dribbling down their chins, and heard their peculiar, grating wails, she felt a kind of panic. Once one of them spit some white lumpy stuff on her shoulder, and she kept smelling the curdled milk even after she laundered the blouse. Finally she gave up and used it as a dust rag. Ivan found a job in a small university town a couple of hours away as associate director of a foundation that gave grants for the visual arts.

And Caroline, through a combination of her contacts, published papers, and notoriety as a female researcher, was hired as an assistant professor in the math department. When they drove out to visit the foundation and the university and to look at houses, their future neighborhood appeared mild, even beneficent. Speeding back along the turnpike to Boston, she asked him, "Do you mind leaving?"

"No."

"I'll miss some of the people."

"We can still see the ones we really like."

"You're very detached, Ivan. Isn't there anything you'll miss?"

"Not much. I've had enough of that sort of life."

It had not been what she expected, either. Except for the very beginning, when they were so close, there had been long stretches of bleakness. Yet the odd thing was, her richest memories were from that time she called bleak, when they would be estranged for long stretches then come together, unaccountably, for days of ineffable common delight, knowing all the while that the delight could fade instantaneously into bleakness again. What she recalled most from their first two years as the happy couple was a vague constraint, like behaving well in school. A too tight embrace. The blankets at night heavy, like straps. Unhappiness loosed them into a manic oscillation, like the needle of their speedometer, which had broken and ran wild. It made the future unimaginable and frightening. No wonder they were weary and sought rest.

"What about Chantal?"

"What about her?" He passed a car, accelerating to possibly seventy-five, though the needle was at twenty. As he grew older he drove more and more furiously. Caroline did not comment—she knew him too well for that—but trusted, a virtue born of necessity.

"Won't you miss her?"

"You'll never get that out of your mind, will you?"

"I don't even mind so much. It's just that you don't say one way or the other."

"You know I'll never say now, don't you?"

"My punishment for asking."

"Did I ever ask you one thing?"

"Never. But then you are a saint. We know that." All very quiet, she thought. So quiet, like after a death.

They stopped on the road for sodas. She watched him standing with his head bent back, tipping the bottle to his mouth. He had worn a suit and tie to meet with the board of directors, but took the tie and jacket off afterwards; his white shirt was open at the neck and the sleeves were rolled up. He was tired, and more and more lately, when he was tired, he wore thick horn-rimmed glasses instead of the contact lenses. They made him look vulnerable, and older. He was still a lean and a young man and still when she looked at him appraisingly, as now, she remembered his touch. But she had an inkling of how he might soon settle into middle age—spreading belly, baggy pants, thinning hair, beefy neck. Her flesh shrank at the idea of some potbellied meaty man crawling all over her. She had never chosen that. She had chosen Ivan as he was then, in Rome. Time, what it would foist on her, was the ultimate unfairness.

At home it depressed them to find the apartment a shambles of half-packed cartons, piles of books and records, dishes and pots. The early morning, when they set out, seemed very long ago. The years spent in that apartment were piled on all sides too, a weighty thickness of time surrounding them. They had a history, and history was more potent, even, than love.

It had turned suddenly hot. Caroline rummaged in a carton to find shorts and a halter. She heated last night's dinner, and they drank cold white wine out of paper cups. Ivan stared at her strangely, long and intense as the very first time, but with a predatory glimmer. He stood up.

"Would you please get up?" he asked.

"What is it?"

"Just stand up. I want to see you."

"But why? I haven't changed."

"I would just like to see you. Can't I see you?"

"Ivan, I . . . I don't like the way you look." She stood up.

"You're very attractive, still. You're right. You haven't changed a bit."

"Attractive" was not his sort of word. "I'm flattered, but what is wrong with you?"

"You know," he said, taking off his glasses—and without the glasses his eyes narrowed in the glare of the uncovered bulbs—"sometimes a certain body has a hold on you, it's a completely irrational thing. At least for a man." He shrugged. "I don't know if it's the same for a woman."

"Are you talking about me?" She looked down at her own body, which seemed slight and harmless.

He took hold of her arm and shook it angrily. "Of course I'm talking about you. Who do you think I'm talking about? You know how many times I almost walked out of this place?"

"What am I supposed to say? Go, then."

"I don't want to go." He pulled her by the arm. "Come closer. I want to . . . Right now."

"Get your hands off me! What kind of a way is that? Let go of me, Ivan!"

He didn't speak. His fingers met around her arm, a tight ring. She remembered that grip from the very beginning, from the afternoon he showed her the wolf.

"Are you going to let me go?"

He shook his head.

"But I don't feel like it. What do you want? Do you want to see me struggle? Is that the game? Or are you out of your mind?"

He just stood there, gripping her arm. She knew him. He could keep that grip all night if he had to. "Okay, Ivan," she said. "Okay. You win. Take your prize. But just wait a minute, all right? Just take it easy, will you?"

"I don't need instructions. Shut your mouth and open your legs."

"Pig!" With her free hand she smacked his face hard.

He shoved her to the floor and grabbed at her shorts. She tried to twist out of his grasp, but it was no use. He didn't wait. It was rough and it hurt. Then he collapsed on her neck and he wept.

"Jesus Christ, will you stop crying? I survived."

"I don't know what happened to me. It must be the move, and . . . everything. God, how could I? I'm sorry."

"All right! It's not as if you're a total stranger."

"Are you okay? Did I hurt you?"

"Yes, and yes. What did you expect?"

"Will you ever forgive me?"

"Stop it, will you? I can't stand you like this."

"What came over me? I'm not that sort of man."

"You can't figure it out? Ask Jerome." He was so heavy a weight on top of her, she could hardly draw a clear breath. "Please move."

"I'm sorry." He moved.

"Stop saying you're sorry. I know you're sorry. Do something."

"Do what?"

"Do something for me now."

"How can you still want me . . . ?"

"I don't know how."

So they had come to this. She had no self left, only flesh, and she felt she might die of it, willingly. How much simpler to die now and not have to live with herself any more. As it faded she remembered the night in Rome when she was filled with panic thinking she would die if she could not have him, and how she had wanted to be obliterated. Now she knew what it felt like to be obliterated. She thought how love, to which she had surrendered, was a loathsome thing. She deserved it.

Ivan wasn't ready to buy a house so they rented one, a small two-story frame house near the university. They spent the money they had saved in Boston filling it with rugs and soft furniture. On questions of style they agreed spontaneously. Ivan found butcher-block tables and enormous pillows and exotic posters, and he went in for plants—before long the living room was a jungle. He hovered over them, touching their leaves solicitously, and when he transferred them from smaller pots to larger ones he held the clumps of earth and roots in his hands the way a midwife receives a slippery, fragile newborn, with reverence.

Since the house had three bedrooms they could each have a separate study—Ivan's sensible idea. Working at her desk in the evenings, Caroline had no one to turn around and talk to for diversion. It was better that way. The loss was easier to bear alone. And she could listen to music now while she worked; Ivan could not work to music.

Inspired partly by the room, which she painted white and furnished sparsely, Caroline resolved to devote herself to her work. Like a nun, she would renounce the joys of family and hearth. The students here were not as dazzling, but they were also not as tensely competitive. Their sense of wonder revived her own. She began an article about knotted spheres in four-space, difficult enough to claim all her attention. Falling asleep, dreaming and waking, she drew pictures of curves in her head; she could dress and scramble eggs and make coffee in utter absence from the physical world. Ivan was nearby, familiar and amenable, someone to eat with and go to an occasional movie with, to bring to math department parties. But she no longer explored him. As she had imagined long ago, the layers were endless, but since she had glimpsed the brutish underside she did not care to uncover anything more. About her own life she thought as little as possible. She saw it as narrowed to a single path where once there had been many, and she traveled it numb and alone. After their night of bestiality on the floor amid the mess of cartons, they mostly let each other alone.

The life they led together was outwardly mild, except for a series of peculiar accidents. Getting up from a chair in the living room one afternoon, Caroline lacerated the cornea of her right eye on a leaf of an avocado plant Ivan had grown from the pit. Gasping in pain, she asked a neighbor to drive her to the emergency room of the hospital. The eye healed, but she said his putting the plant so close to the chair was a deliberate risk. He was sorry it happened, but said the inference was absurd. A while later a small fire downstairs destroyed some notes for his book on the phases of Roman architecture. She must have left a cigarette burning, said Ivan. She was sure she hadn't; it was faulty wiring in the old house. Even the firemen agreed. But Ivan persisted in feeling she had destroyed his book. He had worked on it fitfully for almost seven years, Caroline reminded him; it was not she who had aborted it. Anyhow, he should have kept the notes upstairs in his private study. Ivan raised the seat on her bicycle, using it when his own was broken, and forgot to lower it. Caroline fell, sprained her ankle and walked with a cane for two weeks. Soon after, she used his razor on her legs and left the blade on the rim of the sink. Groping the next morning without his lenses, he sliced a finger. It looked very suspicious, she thought, but they were accidents.

Once more she realized that Ivan, besides being intelligent, was prescient: you can have sex with anyone. Twice with a persuasive French professor, who plied her with home-baked brioches, and many times with her most brilliant graduate student, Mark. Mark was an amiable young man, unexceptional aside from his mathematical wizardry. Sex was not the best part of their affair, at least for Caroline. The best part was relief at being with someone who did not know her so well. He thought he knew her, but young and lacking the imagination of Ivan, he had no idea of all there was to know. She talked to him about her work, which Ivan did not understand, about the vanishing thread in the Minotaur's cave that she still pursued. Late afternoons they sat together on his bed with multicolored pencils and paper, drawing pictures and making conjectures. They were working on a new knot invariant and constructing covering spaces. Mark was a wonderful find: he had flights of algebraic genius, while her flights were geometric. They complemented each other, and together they wrote a paper. She insisted he get top billing, and deliver it at the next conference.

The worst part of their affair was her getting pregnant. Mark arranged for the abortion locally—students knew all about such things—and she paid. There was no question; she cut off at the root any tenderness she might feel for it. This was no child of love, but an unwanted excrescence, like a fungus, to be scraped off her inner walls. Without any anesthesia, she felt her pain as a scraping that made an excruciating sound, like fingernails scraping frost off a window. The pain helped, recalling the pain of the other bizarre accidents, and yanking this one into that orbit of mutual injury, except this one could be caught before it harmed Ivan. There were some injuries too terrible to inflict. In topology, spaces might be infinitely twisted, tugged and pushed, provided that no shapes were snapped in two, or poked with holes, or forced inside out. That was the contract the mathematician accepted. She trusted Ivan would accept the same: no irreparable wounds. The underside of the marriage contract, in invisible ink. So she lied and told him she was going away to a two-day conference on manifold theory, and when he inquired on her return why she seemed so pale and wan, she said she had picked up a stomach virus that was going around.

She was easier with him after, and more companionable, and nearly forgave him for his assault, now that they were even. She could not forget how they had battled on the floor, but she dared to hope that someday she might recall it without shuddering, might even find a tenuous place for it in a large design, as yet invisible. Meanwhile, they spent time together like discreet old friends, avoiding difficult subjects. One evening she had a real stomach virus. Helpless, drained, her flesh like watery dough, she felt the way she imagined people feel when death is near. Her forehead throbbed, she was dizzy and she had just vomited in the bathroom.

Ivan helped her undress and spread the quilt over her gently. "Go to sleep now."

"No." She raised the pillows. "It will be better soon. I want to stay up. No, don't go yet." She caught his hand and pulled him down to sit near her on the bed. "Stay with me awhile. Talk to me. I feel so weak."

She felt more than weak. She felt despair. She was afraid to be alone, afraid to think, for every thought became a pain that wound its way to the pounding center in her head.

"What shall we talk about?"

"I can't talk. You talk. Anything. What did you do today? Tell me. Or tell me a story."

He was silent for a while. When he spoke his voice penetrated, to diffuse warmth from inside her to her chilly skin. "Remember Lucca? Remember when we went to Lucca? We walked around and heard the music in the churches. It was your birthday, the festival of Sant'Anna. Remember?"

She nodded. She remembered. The words made her want to cry. In her weakness, they sounded beautiful, spoken like an incantation. She hadn't expected anything beautiful. Tears might release the awful tightness in her head, but she didn't want to cry while he was there. She pressed his hand.

"Remember we walked on the walls of the city?" Ivan said. "Stone walls encircling the city. It was raining, soft gray rain. The festival of Sant'Anna, your birthday. We walked on the walls in the rain. We saw Lucca. Remember? It was your birthday."

"I remember," she whispered. Saint Anne was the patron saint of pregnant women, a man in the tobacco shop had told her, while Ivan waited on the street. What was it like, a baby kicking around inside? Probably like the stomach cramps, an inner tormentor.

"Lucca." He paused. His eyes were far away, seeing rain on the stone walls. "Are you crying, Caroline?"

"No. It's nothing. I remember Lucca very well. I had forgotten." She held his hand in hers, spread out his fingers and touched them, one by one. "Tell me some more about that trip."

She was empty, waiting for him to fill her up, feed her with memories. He was silent again, then he laughed. "Remember Arezzo? There we were both sick. God, how sick we were."

"We stayed in that little room for three days."

"Yes. First I got sick and you took care of me, then we were both sick, then I got better and took care of you. We couldn't eat anything. We just lay in bed and groaned."

"We had them send up tea sometimes."

"Yes. Remember how they looked at us? And the boy who brought up the tea? He wore knickers. They thought we were on our honeymoon. We didn't leave the room for three days."

"Finally we went out," she said.

"Yes. You were embarrassed to pass by the desk."

"We told them we'd been sick but they didn't look like they believed us."

"Then we walked, and we went to that restaurant up the hill and ate chicken soup with noodles. Our first meal."

"I remember that," Caroline said. "We pretended it was a feast."

"Yes." He held her hand in both of his and stroked it absent-mindedly. "Do you feel a little better now?"

She could tell he wanted to go back to his desk. "A little better. Tell me once more about Lucca, then I'll let you go."

"The second time around, you know, nothing sounds as good."

"Just tell me."

"Lucca. It was raining. A gray soft rain. We walked on the walls in the rain. It was your birthday, the festival of Sant'Anna. We held hands and walked. We heard the singing in the churches. Their voices—remember—were high and glorious, streaming upward, as if they could make the sun come out. You remember Lucca, Caroline, as well as I do."

They could never part, she and Ivan. They were locked

together, locked in the memory of Lucca. She let her hand fall out of his to the blanket.

He stood up and kissed her forehead, then turned out the light.

"No. Leave the light on."

"Don't you want to sleep? You look so pale."

"I may sleep. But leave it on. I don't want the dark."

"All right." He turned the light on. "Call me if you need anything."

Lucca was a dream. Shifting around carefully, Caroline found a position, lying on her side with a pillow propped near her stomach, that made her body feel no longer there, anesthetized.

Besides beautiful, he could still be funny, he could be gallant, he could be intriguing, if she would accept these gifts. On a Sunday in early spring he came up with an intriguing idea. They were having hero sandwiches and Chianti on a blanket spread on the small back lawn. Ivan's daffodils had just sprung: the square of grass was rimmed with shimmering gold.

"If I play my cards right," he said, "and work through the summer, I can arrange to have about six weeks off next fall."

"That's terrific. You could certainly use a long vacation. You work so hard."

"I thought maybe we could take a trip."

"But it's right in the middle of the semester."

"I thought we might go to Rome."

"Rome!" She looked up. Her hand, raising a glass, stopped in midair. "Oh, I wish I could."

"Do it, then. Take the semester off."

"How can I? It's not even two years. I'm not due for a sabbatical for ages."

"Just take it without pay. Don't ask them, tell them. Personal reasons."

"They're not keen on personal reasons."

"Listen, you've made yourself practically indispensable there, especially with the tutoring program. They're getting a bargain and they know it. Don't worry, I know how these things work. I'll tell you exactly how to go about it."

He would. He knew how everything worked, and he would plan the perfect strategy for her. He should have gone into politics, only he was too reticent and would despise campaigning. "You really think . . . ?" she said.

"Did I ever lead you astray?" With a cavalier flourish that recalled his younger self, he raised the straw-covered bottle.

"It's too early to say," she replied, holding out the wineglasses for him.

"Well, think about it, anyway."

It was unlikely that they would fire her. With women making faint noises about professional inequities, it was an unpropitious time to let one go, especially one who could be outspoken and had credentials in so exotic a field as topology. The two graduate seminars could be deferred. As for the undergraduate courses—a stroke of genius: she would recommend Mark. It would lift his spirits—she had avoided him since the abortion—and it was safe. Mark was more than competent for the job, but not sufficiently entrenched to take it from her. Ah, she thought, drinking the wine, such fiendish tactics were not native to her. They had seeped in through Ivan.

"You have a devilish grin," Ivan said. "What is it?"

"Just figuring," she replied. "Just figuring. Oh, but we have hardly any money left. The house. How are we going to manage it?" They had recently bought the house. Ivan decided after a year and a half that it was foolish to keep paying rent; they should make an investment and build up equity.

"We'll do it very cheaply." He smiled. "Remember how to do it cheaply, Caroline?" A breeze ruffled the grass. The daffodils swayed this way and that in unison, like a row of dancers. Ivan reached out to pick a flower and put it behind her ear. "Remember?" he said, and his eyes, green and shining, held in untouched completeness the memory of everything that had happened in Rome, so that gazing into them, it was as if the surface of an ocean had become transparent and she saw all the buried treasure beneath, as well as hope, and the risk engendered by despair.

Ivan could hardly wait to see his old street. It was morning and the doors to La Taverna Romanaccia were closed, but the sign still beckoned, faded and a little dingy. Four filled garbage cans stood at the side door from which the horse used to emerge every night. Clusters of flies buzzed around them. Ivan's ancient five-story building was the same—shuttered windows, broken cornice and spotted façade—as were the other weathered stone buildings on the square. The only difference was more people, a steady stream of them, all going in the same direction. Following, they found a large new five-and-ten-cent store around the corner and down half a block. Ivan frowned at the display of plastic household articles in the window. Then back at his front door, he said, "I bet she's not here any more. Look." He pointed down to the two marble steps at the entrance, dulled and marked with the scraping of many feet.

"She may be getting old," said Caroline.

"No, she'd never let them get this way." They stepped into the outer hall with its rows of mailboxes, unpolished. The paint was peeling and the floor was dusty. An empty Stop cigarette pack lay crushed in a corner. The inner door was locked. Ivan was morose as they went back out.

The *portiera* of the next building appeared carrying a string bag and, like Signora Daveglio, dressed in black, but without an apron. She was slight, with sparse white hair and soft features. Ivan stopped her. She did not remember him, but at the word "Fulbright" she gave an "Ah!" of recognition and smiled broadly. In answer to his questions she produced a swift flow of inflected words, and spreading her palms to the heavens, shook her head from side to side sadly. As she gazed toward Ivan's building she repeatedly made a rolling, descending motion with one arm. Waves in the sea? thought Caroline. The ceaseless flow of life? Something like that. Ivan thanked her and she walked briskly off in the direction of the new store.

"Well?"

"She had a heart attack about two years ago," said Ivan. "Very sudden. That was it."

"Really? How did it happen?"

"You'll never guess."

"Scrubbing the stairs?"

"Very good. *Preciso.* She was at the top and she keeled right over. The pail spilled with her. The building has been going downhill every since."

"She kicked the bucket," said Caroline.

"That's right." They were at the corner. Ivan turned to look at the building once more, shading his eyes against the glare of the sun. "The Communist Party has lost a loyal supporter."

"She liked you a lot too."

"Yes. She used to bake me these little pastries sometimes and bring them up after supper, to have while I was working. *Sfogliatelle,* they were called. They were very delicate, very light. That was before you came along."

"I never knew she baked."

"Yes, she was a great baker. Oh well," he sighed.

They walked to the river. "Over there"—he pointed—"is the Castel Sant'Angelo. A fortress. Did I ever tell you? The Renaissance Popes used to take refuge . . ."

She listened politely, but she had heard it before. She had heard all that before.

Later, leaning against the balustrade, she said, "You know what I'd like to do, Ivan? I'd like to have dinner in that restaurant, Romanaccia."

"What on earth for?"

"Just to see what it's like. Don't you ever have that feeling—you've looked at something from the outside for so long, you'd like to see what it's like inside?"

"I know exactly what it's like inside. Noisy, a long wait, the waiters snicker at you, the food looks better than it tastes, and they probably have the menu translated in some sort of quaint English."

"Still," said Caroline.

"Oh, all right, if that's what you really want."

At night under the garish lights the dingy old sign looked jolly. Signora Daveglio was not outside in her club sweater reading *l'Unità,* but the horse was there, with its red pompons, and so was the Renaissance man.

"Do you think it's the same horse?"

"How could it be, Ivan? It's close to seven years. It's not even the same Renaissance man."

"No, this one is younger and taller. But he has the same costume."

"You'd still like the costume?"

"If I had known they needed a new Renaissance man I would have flown over and applied."

The restaurant was low-ceilinged and lit with yellow globes. Its red stucco walls were hung with paintings in the style of Caravaggio—faces miming intense emotion in lurid contrasts of dark and light. Interspersed were paintings of the ruins of the Forum and the Colosseum. The wooden tables were crowded with Germans and Swedes with loud voices. The waiters spoke English to the Swedes and to Ivan and Caroline. "A Martini or a Manhattan before dinner, *signore?*" Ivan asked for Campari and soda in Italian. On the menu the prices were outrageous, and below each dish, in parentheses, was a translation in quaint English.

"Oh, look at this." Caroline laughed. " 'Noddles' for noodles. 'The large noddles covered in anchovies and a sauce of garlic, oil of olive, and parsleys.' And look how they spell asparagus!"

Ivan glared.

The accordion broke out, a gaseous sound slurping and gulping through a rampaging arpeggio.

She hoped the accordionist would not play the tune. That would be sacrilegious. She remembered the curve of the tune precisely, though she had never learned its name and had never heard it played since the night they crossed the square with Signora Daveglio's eyes boring into their backs, after Ivan made love to her on the lumpy mattress on the floor and said he wanted to marry her so she would always be there, and that they would not become like other married people. Ivan hummed it sometimes, but he hummed it off key.

The accordionist, approaching their table and drowning out the sound of human voices, was playing *"Là ci darem la mano,"* from *Don Giovanni.* Caroline knew it well. Don Giovanni was trying to persuade the innocent peasant, Zerlina, to sneak off with him. He says he wants to marry her, *"Quest' istante."* This instant. In the opera the melody was sweetly and irresistibly seductive. *"Vorrei e non vorrei,"* she says. I want, I don't want. *"Io cangierò tua sorte!"* I'll change your destiny. *Presto, non son più forte!"* Quick then, I have no more strength. *"Vieni! Vieni!"* Come! But this accordionist was jazzing it up, converting the smooth lyrical line into a dinky common beat that unmasked the self-seeking Don, the fine lord, so that anyone, even the gullible Zerlina, would know enough not to trust his words. At last he passed on to other tables. The food, when it was finally brought, looked better than it tasted.

"I should never have let you persuade me," said Ivan.

"Why don't you just make the best of it?"

They did not linger. On the way out they squeezed past a party of Japanese men with cameras hanging from straps around their necks. Ivan stopped to give a few coins to the Renaissance man and Caroline patted the horse.

Ivan read in a magazine that thirty-five miles north of Rome was an outdoor hot spring sulfur bath, with swimming year round. *Andiamo,* he said. Let's go! This spree in chilly November put them in an antic mood. In the rented Fiat Ivan played with the gearshift and explored the dashboard while giving a dramatic reading of passages from the operator's manual. In his literal translation it became a zany comic text that had Caroline breathless with laughter. When they tried to adjust the seats, they bumped knees and heads and giggled wildly, and she had a fleeting vision of the two of them young and carefree forever, through a lifetime of madcap jaunts. Why couldn't it always be this way? Whatever was wrong had vanished for the moment. Ivan must have felt the same, for out on the open road he put his hand over hers. "It's not so bad, is it? With us, I mean? We're having a good time."

She clasped his hand.

First they smelled it, then they saw it. From outside, the bath was an austere rectangular building of whitish brick. They entered and reluctantly they parted—Caroline into the women's dressing room, Ivan into the men's—to meet again at the pool, shivering. The sky was bone white. The only other patrons were two stout elderly people who stood, immersed to the waist, at opposite ends of the pool. The man, whose sagging chest was covered with white hair, rubbed water over his flabby arms and shoulders.

"This is crazy!" Caroline said. "I'm freezing. And it stinks! Are you sure we should do it?"

"It's warm in there. Come on. Time for your bath." He yanked at her with both hands, teasing and pulling her to the edge of the pool.

"Don't push me in! Don't you dare!" she cried. "I'll go myself." She dived in. The water was warm. A steamy smell of decayed matter rose from the surface. Ivan dived in after her and came up pushing the long drenched hair back from his forehead.

"Doesn't this feel terrific?"

"Yes, but what is that awful stuff floating around?" She pointed. There were blobs of it all over the pool. "It looks like shit."

"That's the sulfur, silly. That's what's supposed to do you so much good."

"It still looks like shit. Floating shit."

"Would you care to try some?" Ivan took a blob in his hand and came towards her.

"Get away from me with that! Yuk!" She fled underwater and darted away.

With impassive faces, the old people at their opposite ends watched them romping in the water. The white-chested man rubbed water incessantly over his arms and shoulders. The woman, whose broad face thrust forth from her yellow rubber cap as from a medieval wimple, lay on her back from time to time and floated without moving her arms or legs. When she began to sink she would right herself, and stare for a while before floating again. Coming up after a dive, Caroline saw two new people, a man and a woman huddled close together near the far edge of the pool, with their backs to her. Boy and girl, really, from the looks of them. He was stocky and curly-haired. She wore a black and white zebra-striped bikini, and her dark hair was coiled on top of her head and held in place by a barrette. She took a few steps away from the pool. For a slender, tall girl she moved with an odd heaviness. Her body didn't click into position with the jauntiness of young women in bikinis. Her stance was odd too, tilted back and slightly arched. Ivan swam up behind Caroline and put his arms around her waist under the water. The boy put his arm around the girl and whispered in her ear. She turned around. She was hugely pregnant. The skin between the top and the bottom of her bikini formed a sphere tautly filled and stretched. Her belly button had popped out.

"*Madonna!* Is that the latest fashion?" asked Ivan.

Caroline smiled too, but her eyes had drifted out of focus. Everything blurred. The water, up to her breasts, felt suddenly hot.

The boy kept whispering and nudging at the girl, who kept turning away and retreating.

"Do you know who she looks like?" Caroline said. "Remember that woman Rusty, and Ed? The ones who left the baby alone? She has that same petrified look."

"Yes, a little. I wonder what ever happened to that baby."

"Suffocated, no doubt."

Finally the young couple entered the pool from the shallow end. He held her arm going down the slippery steps. She swam off quickly, her long thin arms attacking the water, while the boy came over and began talking in a confidential way to Ivan. Smiling paternally, Ivan answered in a reassuring tone, and soon the boy grinned a farewell and swam away.

"What was that all about?" Caroline asked.

"She didn't want to go in because she was embarrassed. She thought there wouldn't be anyone else here on a Thursday morning. There usually isn't. She didn't bother to get the right kind of bathing suit because they're expensive and ugly and in a month or so she'll have her baby."

"Oh."

Ivan smoothed down her hair with long strokes. Under the water he ran his fingers along her bare sides, down her ribs, over her hips. He came closer, his eyes admiring. "Now you, in a bikini, are a splendid sight to behold."

She turned away. "It's all right, Ivan, really. You don't have to."

He swam off underwater, out of sight.

From opposite ends of the pool the old stout couple swam slowly toward the center, where they met and walked side by side to the shallow end. They climbed the steps in silence, wrapped white towels around their shoulders, and walked in silence to the exit, where they parted, she to the women's section and he to the men's. Caroline watched them disappear. She picked up a piece of the brown, porous sulfur floating nearby. It was light and papery, not solid as it appeared. It didn't feel pleasant, but it was bearable to hold. Slippery and scummy, it draped itself around her open hand.

They tried to pick up their antic mood but it felt forced. The day was spoiled.

Since Caroline had never been south, they traveled into the Apennines, which Ivan said had a primitive, stark beauty. But on the way there was a mountain snowstorm, and they had to creep along a narrow road behind a snow plow for three hours. In Paestum they took an unheated room overnight to save money. It was November, but the snow was days behind them, and southern Italy was a warm place, they thought. The afternoon had been warm and drenched in sun, with the temple columns turning golden in the early twilight. Hours later a deep, dark midnight cold set in, an arctic cold. The air was thick with it. It crept inside their bones and nestled in their inner organs. Caroline's nose was running. She forced herself to get up for one of Ivan's handkerchiefs, but could hardly grasp it in her shivering fingers. She tossed their light coats over the blankets and brought their bathrobes back to bed with her. Even in fragments of sleep they kept the memory of cold; their dreams transmuted the theme of cold. Ivan moaned softly to himself. At about three in the morning he had an idea: there was hot water—they could take a shower. They fooled around for a while in the shower, tossing washcloths, but back under the blankets they froze again, waiting for dawn in grim silence, each resenting the other for having chosen the unheated room. In the morning the sun streamed in. Why didn't we make love to get warm? Caroline thought, opening the windows wide. Why didn't one of us suggest that? Was it just too cold for that?

All this put them out of sorts, yet they tried to be considerate, like traveling companions thrown together by war or natural disaster. Caroline missed her work. In the middle of the night she woke in strange rooms obsessed by a problem she had left unfinished, involving a higher-dimensional knot. If only she were alone in her office with a pencil and blank paper. She had purposely left all her notes and pictures at home, and now regretted it. There was little she could do in the dark but ravel and unravel what was already accomplished. In daylight there was too much space to think. While Ivan raced around the hairpin turns she shut her eyes and thought about her life in broad, difficult ways, what she was doing, and how, and to what purpose, ways she hadn't thought since the bleakest moments of her despair. She thought about great imponderables like hope and time and injustice, destiny and death, but her mind was not accustomed to such blurry ascents and she fell back repeatedly. She was trained for the exquisite conjectures of mathematics, which fitted the fine intricacies of her brain like microscopic tongues in microscopic grooves. She loved these conjectures, even though she knew that in the course of daily human life they did not matter. It was precisely for their gratuitousness that she loved them. The larger questions mattered a great deal, and she feared she was missing them somehow, as ancient weavers working on a segment of tapestry missed the grand design. Ivan was not missing them. With his lateral vision and his feel for history he was seeing them and suffering them in his veiled way. Because of her? Was she his useful paradigm of the obstacles of the world? Or in spite of her? Or was she irrelevant to what he was suffering, to his experience of life? Too inconsequential, a nuisance? Maybe she should get out of his way, then, and let him live and suffer in peace.

They returned to Rome two weeks later, at nine in the evening, to find the lobby of their small hotel deserted. Ivan rapped on the front desk and called, *"C'è nessuno?"*

The gray-haired owner rushed out from the small apartment off the lobby. *"Gli americani,"* he turned and called back. *"Sono tornati."*

His wife, the *padrona,* rushed out too, followed by the bellboy and the chambermaid. They were all shouting. The *padrona* was in tears.

"Signore, signora," she cried, running to them.

"Ma che c'è?" Ivan asked, setting down the bags.

The Italians encircled them with horrified faces.

"Il presidente, il vostro presidente Kennedy è morto," the woman wailed.

"Oh no," said Caroline.

"Sì sì, è vero! Assassinato."

The six of them crowded into the owners' tiny living room to watch television. The *padrone* poured out six small glasses of a colorless, sharp-smelling liqueur. Anisette; it stung. The television coverage was live from the States— Ivan translated for the Italians. The instant of violence was replayed again and again: the President had a ragged hole in the side of his head, his wife's skirt was spattered with blood. Not long ago, Caroline remembered, she had lost a baby too. The Italians cried, but Caroline and Ivan were too stunned to cry. The *padrona* brought out bread and cheese. No matter what happened, she said, people had to eat. During the war, during the Occupation, during the horrors, they always remembered that they had to eat to keep up their strength, though good food was scarce then. On the mantelpiece were framed photographs of three young people. The younger son was off working in Switzerland, their host explained through his tears, their daughter was married and living in Turin, and the oldest son had been killed in the war, by the Germans.

When, two days later, they walked past the American Embassy, a classical white building set back from the street on a bright green lawn, they found the high gates barred. Locked outside, Americans stood about quietly in clusters of twos and threes. Caroline and Ivan stood for a moment with them and walked on. A block away vendors were hawking their newspapers, shouting words Caroline could not understand. People rushed over to snatch up the papers.

"What could it be this time?"

"I can't make it out. We'll see." Ivan bought a paper and leaned against a lamppost to read. "The man who they say shot Kennedy was shot himself. In jail."

"It can't be, Ivan. Calm down and read it again."

He read it again, and showed her the picture on the front page. "That's it. It's what I said." His face was slack and drawn. They had not slept. "My eyes hurt," he said, handing her the paper. "Hold this. I want to take out my lenses."

They left early, no longer in a holiday mood. Pacing and muttering, Ivan tossed his clothes into the open suitcase on the bed. "Now we're in for it," he groaned. "Now we're really in for it. Before was bad enough, but now . . ."

"A *brutto periodo.*"

He turned on her furiously. "Will you please stop saying that stupid phrase? Do you have to trivialize everything?"

"I'm sorry."

"I'm sorry, Caroline. I'm upset."

"No, you're right. It was a stupid thing to say. I'm sorry."

They stared at each other, piles of clothing in their arms. "This is ridiculous," said Ivan.

Yes, it was. Now they were in for it, she thought. They were really in for it, because it was clear that this marriage had nowhere to go. Over. End of an era: *presto,* swear in the next life before the body cooled. Shocked out of numbness, she found she was exhausted by grief. *Non son più forte.* She couldn't hang on any more. For what? His ploy of rekindling from nostalgia had failed. They came for nostalgia but they got horror. She had been through all the ugly spells she had strength for. Nothing lasted. Even an elected emblem of stability . . . Look at him, a hole in his head, brains all over his wife's skirt. Crowds weeping. Surely she could face so small a shattering, in the scheme of things, as leaving Ivan.

Late as usual, they boarded the plane out of breath, with the engines already whirring. Ivan had left a book in the hotel and insisted on dashing back. As they took off Caroline was making plans. She could get an apartment. He could keep the house and the car. He could have the TV. He could have the furniture. There wasn't much she needed, only the phonograph and records—he didn't care about music. She could live simply, like a Quaker or a hermit. A mattress on the floor. Ironic, how Ivan had turned out to be the one with accumulations—plants, books, magazines, prints, ties. She bore him no malice; she liked Ivan a lot. They could be friends. How banal, how unoriginal: they could be friends! But sooner or later everyone's destiny was banal. Why strive to be forever original? It was arrogance. Even an arrogance as finely wrought as Kennedy's could be shot down in broad daylight by an ignominious gunman, not even an anarchist.

They expected to find the country in a shambles, but everything was running smoothly. Disturbingly smoothly. They unpacked, Caroline got back to her higher-dimensional knot, Ivan collected his plants from the neighbors. She called Mark to see how the courses were going. No, she didn't want to meet for lunch, but if he had any trouble he could get in touch. There was no hurry about her leaving. They were both shaken up, Ivan more practically so because a change in presidents meant a change in tone and eventually, as waterfalls trickle out into rills, a change in the flow of money for the arts. When things calmed down she would announce her plans. Meanwhile, winter came and she returned to work. A smooth ease settled over her, now that she had accepted her unoriginal fate. The pervasive bleakness of the land seemed to relieve her of private bleakness, and knowing her life with him was temporary, she began to regard Ivan from a great distance, to think of him in strangely objective ways. He is really a very good-looking man, she would think. He is really a very intelligent man. And very good-natured too. How fortunate to have known so fine a man so intimately. Such thoughts in their absurd formal expression, as if he were dead, made her smile to herself. Ivan caught her at it in the supermarket.

"What are you grinning at?"

She decided to tell the truth, silly as it was, since it was all over anyway. "I was thinking of your vocabulary, when you write. You use a lot of good words. I mean, sort of picturesque words."

"Oh, come off it, Caroline."

"No, really, I'm quite serious. Like the review you did last month. That book about the origins of Art Nouveau. That was a really good review. I liked the words. Tracery. Aperture. Patina."

"They're not so remarkable. If you read a lot of other criticism you'd see. In fact patina's gotten too common."

"Maybe. But still, to get them all in one paragraph . . ."

He pushed the cart along with a shrug. But she could tell he was silently pleased, and confused.

She was waiting for him after work, standing under the movie marquee watching others buy their tickets. Ten minutes. Fifteen minutes. Her blood raced with indignation. He was later and later every year, pathological; he didn't want to be anywhere he had promised to be. Appointments, even, were coercive! He was crazy! She worked out a lateness coefficient and started to calculate what proportion of her life had been spent waiting for him, and how correspondingly good it would be soon, very very soon, never to wait again. With the figures multiplying in her head, she looked absently at the clusters of people approaching the main intersection a block away. At the corner they stopped as a body and waited for the light. A man caught her eye, who had detached himself from the crowd and paused to look at a display of books on an outdoor table. His profile was partly hidden from her, but she could see that he was tall and lean, and he wore a corduroy jacket. She liked the concentrated way he stood there, wrapped in a private calm, as though he could never be late and in a rush, never overworked, never taciturn. He inspired the first visceral flicker she had felt for a man in some time. Ah yes, someone like that. When he turned from the books to cross the street in a confident, unhurried stride, her first impulse was to laugh at herself. But on second thought it was not at all funny. He bent to kiss her on the cheek. "Sorry I'm late. I had to finish something up, and then the bus was so slow that I got out and dashed over. Did it start yet?"

In the movie she reached for his hand. He put her hand on his knee and held it there, the way he used to at the many movies they had gone to in earlier times. This was an Italian film about love and politics, something for everyone. As the couple on the screen embraced Ivan put his arm around her. She leaned her head against his shoulder. In the public darkness they performed mild rituals of touching that she remembered from high school, tentative gestures ventured by tentative children who knew each other only slightly, emboldened by the dark. When they came out there was still a vestige of light in the west. They faced each other on the street, blinking. Caroline was overcome with desire. He stroked her cheek slowly, perusing her.

"Do you want to go out to dinner?" he asked. "Or home?"

"Home."

They were caught up in a rush of passion that went on for weeks. And why not indulge it, since it would all be over soon? They were not talking about their angers and failures, working out differences and devising compromises as friends did who went to marriage counselors, a procedure Ivan regarded with disdain. They were at each other like cats. They confessed that they felt old and lecherous and didn't care, they had been through too much to care. In this rampant excess, born of the loss of faith and with no reasonable future, Caroline became pregnant. She was thirty-one years old.

Afterwards she liked to say that she had known the moment it happened. It felt different, she told Ivan, like a pin pricking a balloon, but without the shattering noise, without the quick collapse. "Oh, come on," he said. "That's impossible."

But she had dealt for so long with infinitesimal precise abstractions, and she did know how it happened. The baby was conceived one late-September night, Indian summer. All day the sun had glowed hot and low in the sky, settling an amber torpor on people and things, and the night was the same, only now a dark hot heaviness sank slowly down. The scent of the still-blooming honeysuckle rose to their bedroom window. Just as she was bending over to kiss him, heavy and quivering with heat like the night, he teased her about something—could she spare the time from her latest paper on link groups?—and she punched him lightly on the shoulder. In response Ivan stretched out on her back like a blanket, smothering her, while she struggled beneath, writhing to escape. It was a wordless, sweaty struggle, punctuated with wild laughter, shrieks and gasping breaths. She tried biting but he evaded her, and she tried scratching the fists that held her down, but she couldn't reach. All her desire was transformed into physical effort, yet he was still too strong for her. She refused to say she gave up and he wouldn't loosen his grip, so they lay locked and panting in a static embrace.

"You win," she said at last. As he rolled off she jabbed him in the ribs with her elbow.

"Aha!" Ivan shouted, ready to begin again, but she distracted him. Once the wrestling was at an end she found pleasure tinged with resentment. And later, when they were covered with sweat, dripping on each other, she said, "You don't play fair."

"I don't play fair! Look who's talking."

"It isn't fair that you should always win."

Ivan laughed gloatingly and curled up in her arms. She smiled in the dark.

That was the night the baby was conceived, not in high passion but rough strife.

When she phoned him at work after seeing the doctor, he was incredulous. He came home beaming foolishly, and when they wanted to make love, he asked, "Do you think it's all right to do this?"

"Oh, Ivan, honestly. It's microscopic."

He was in one of his whimsical moods and made terrible jokes that she laughed at with easy indulgence. He said he was going to pay the baby a visit and asked if she had any messages she wanted delivered. He unlocked from her embrace, moved down her body and said he was going to have a look for himself. Clowning, he put his ear between her legs to listen. Finally he stopped his antics as she clasped her arms around him and whispered, "Ivan, you are really too silly." He became unusually gentle. Tamed, and she didn't like it, hoped he wouldn't continue that way for months. "Ivan," she explained patiently, "you know, it really is all right. I mean, it's a natural process."

"Well, I didn't want to hurt you."

"I'm not sick."

Then, as though her body were admonishing that cool assurance, she did get sick, with a paralyzing nausea that resembled violent hunger. Mornings, she had to ask Ivan to bring her a hard roll from the kitchen before she could risk stirring from bed. Something needed to be filled, a menacing vacuum occupying her insides. The crucial act was getting the first few mouthfuls down. With enough roll inside to stabilize her, she could sometimes manage a half-cup of tea, but liquids were risky. They sloshed around inside and made her envision the baby sloshing around in its cloudy fluid.

The mornings that she taught were agony. Ivan woke her early, brought her a roll, and gently prodded her out of bed.

"I simply cannot do it." She placed her legs cautiously over the side of the bed.

"Sure you can. Anyhow, you have no choice. You have a job." He was freshly showered and dressed, and his alertness irritated her. She rose to her feet and swayed.

Ivan looked alarmed. "Do you want me to call and tell them you can't make it?"

"No, no." That frightened her. She needed to hold on to the job, to defend herself against the growing baby. Once in the classroom she would be fine. With waves of nausea roiling in her chest, she stumbled into the bathroom.

She liked him to wait until she was out of the shower before he left for work, because she imagined herself fainting under the impact of the water. At the end she forced herself to stand under an ice-cold flow, leaning her head way back and letting her hair drip down behind her. It was torture, but when it was over she felt more alive.

After the shower had been off awhile Ivan would come and open the bathroom door. "Are you okay now, Caroline? I've got to get going."

He kissed her lips, her bare damp shoulder, gave a parting squeeze to her toweled behind, and was gone. She watched him walk down the hall with some trepidation, hoping she wouldn't have to carry a large, inflexible baby. She used to pride herself on strength. When they moved from Boston she had worked as hard as Ivan, lugging furniture and heavy cartons. He was impressed. Now it took all her strength to move her own weight.

Very slowly she would put on clothes, keeping her hard roll nearby and examining her body in the full-length mirror through the stages of dressing. Naked, then in bra and underpants, then with shoes added, and finally with a dress, she looked for signs, but nothing was changed yet. With the profound narcissism of women past first youth, she admired her still-narrow waist and full breasts. She was especially fond of her shoulders and prominent collarbone, which seemed fragile and inviting. That would be all gone soon, gone soft. She scanned her face for the pregnant look she knew well from the faces of friends. It was an intangible change, a membrane of transparent vulnerability that layered the face; a pleading look, a beg for help like a message from a powerless invaded country to the rest of the world. It was not on her face yet.

From the tenth to the fourteenth week she slept, with brief intervals of lucidity when she taught her classes. She had to put aside the paper on link groups. It was an eerie, dreamy time. The nausea faded, but the lure of sleep became potent. In the middle of the day, even, she could pass by the bedroom, glimpse the waiting bed, and be overcome by a soft, heavy desire to lie down. She fell into a stupor immediately and did not dream. She forgot what it was like to awaken with energy and move through an entire day without lying down once. She forgot the feeling of eyes opened wide without effort. She would have liked to hide this strange, shameful perversity from Ivan, but that was impossible. Ivan kept wanting to go to the movies. Clearly, he was bored with her. Maybe he would become so bored he would abandon her and the baby and she would not be able to support the house alone, and she and the baby would end up on the streets in rags, begging. But of course that was highly unlikely.

"You go on, Ivan. I just can't."

One night he said, "I thought I might ask Ruth Forbes to go with me to see the Charlie Chaplin film on High Street. I know she likes him. Would that bother you?"

She was half asleep, slowly eating a large apple in bed and watching *Perry Mason* on television. "No, of course not." Ruth Forbes lived down the block, a casual friend and not Ivan's type at all, too large and loud, divorced and depressed. Caroline didn't care if he wanted her company. She didn't care if he held her hand on his knee in the movies, or even if, improbably, he made love to her afterwards in her sloppy house crawling with children. She didn't care about anything except staying nestled in bed.

She made love with him sometimes, in a slow way. She felt no specific desire but didn't want to refuse him. It was painless, and she could sleep right after. Usually there would be a moment when she came alive despite herself, when the reality of his body inspired a wistful throb of lust, but mostly she was too tired to see it through, to leap towards it, so she let it subside, grateful for the sign of dormant life. She felt sorry for Ivan, but helpless.

Once she fell asleep while he was inside her. He woke her with a pat on her jaw. Actually, she realized from the faint sting, it was more of a slap than a pat. "Caroline, for Chrissake, you're sleeping."

"No, no, I'm sorry. I wasn't really sleeping. Oh, Ivan, it's nothing. This will end." She wondered, though.

Moments later she felt his hands on her thighs. His lips were brooding on her stomach, edging down with expertise. He was murmuring something she couldn't catch. She felt an ache, an irritation. Wryly, she appreciated his intentions, but she couldn't bear that excitement now.

"Please," she said. "Please don't do that."

He was very hurt. He said nothing, leaped away violently and pulled all the blankets around him. She was contrite, but fell instantly into a dreamless dark.

Right after New Year's, when classes were beginning again for the next semester, she woke early and dashed briskly into the shower. She was brushing her teeth with energy when she grasped what had happened. There she was on her feet, sturdy, before eight in the morning, planning how she would introduce the differential calculus to her new students. She stared at her face in the mirror, her mouth dripping white foam, her eyes wide and startled. She was alive! She didn't know how the miracle had happened, nor did she care to explore it. With shocked elation, she zipped up her tight slacks and checked in the mirror. No sign yet. For the moment, she was a survivor.

"Ivan, time to get up."

He grunted and opened his eyes. When they focused on her leaning over him, they darkened with astonishment. He rubbed a fist across his forehead. "Are you dressed already?"

"Yes. Guess what. I'm slept out. I've come back to life."

"Oh." He moaned and rolled over in one piece like a seal.

"Aren't you getting up?"

"In a little while. I'm so tired. I must sleep for a while." The words were thick and slurred.

She was strangely annoyed. Ivan always got up with vigor. "Are you sick?"

"Uh-uh."

He was tired for a week. Caroline wanted to go out every evening—the January air was crisp and exhilarating. But all Ivan wanted to do was lie on the bed and watch prize-fighting movies on television with a can of beer in his hand, like the *New Yorker* cartoons he laughed at. Could this be Ivan? Was it some sort of atavism? It was repellent. Sloth, she pointed out to him, was one of the seven deadly sins. The fifth night she said in exasperation, "What the hell is the matter with you? If you're sick go to a doctor."

"I'm not sick. I'm tired. Can't I be tired too? Leave me alone. I left you alone, didn't I?"

"Ah, but you're much better at that than I am," she snapped. "You have more experience."

One evening soon after Ivan's symptoms disappeared, they sat reading the paper in opposite corners of the living room sofa, her legs stretched diagonally across his. Caroline touched her stomach.

"Ivan."

"What?"

"It's no use. I'm going to have to buy some maternity clothes."

He put down the paper to stare, looking distressed. "Really?"

"Yes."

"Well, don't buy any of those ugly things they wear. Can't you get some of those, you know, sort of Indian things?"

She laughed. "Okay. That's not a bad idea. I will."

He picked up the paper again.

"It moves."

"What?"

"I said it moves. The baby."

"It moves?"

She laughed again. "Remember Galileo? *Eppur si muove.*" They had visited Galileo's birthplace in Pisa, on the way back from Lucca. He was a hero to both of them because he kept his mind free even though his body succumbed to tyranny.

Ivan laughed too. *"Eppur si muove.* Let me feel it." He touched, then looked up at her, his face full of longing, marvel, and envy. In a moment he was scrambling at her clothes in a young, eager rush. He wanted to be there, he said, please, now. She was taken by surprise, on the floor, in silence; it was swift and consuming.

Ivan lay spent in her arms. Caroline, still gasping and clutching him, said, "There's no one like you. I could never love it as much as I love you." She marveled then, hearing her words fall in the still air, that after everything, this could be so. When the baby was born, would it be so?

But after she began wearing the Indian shirts and dresses, Ivan appeared to forget about the baby. When she moaned in bed sometimes, "Oh, I can't get to sleep, it keeps moving around," he responded with a grunt or not at all. He asked her, one Sunday in March, if she wanted to go bicycle riding.

"Ivan, I can't go bike riding. I mean, look at me."

"Oh, right. Of course."

He seemed to avoid looking at her, and she did look awful, she had to admit. Besides the grotesque belly, her ankles swelled up; the shape of her legs was alien. She took diuretics and woke every hour at night to go to the bathroom. Sometimes it was impossible to get back to sleep, so she sat up in bed reading. Ivan said, "Can't you turn the light out? You know I can't sleep with the light on."

"But what should I do? I can't sleep at all."

"Read in the living room."

"It's so cold in there at night."

He turned away irritably. A few times he took the blanket and went to sleep in the living room himself.

When they drove out to picnic in the country on warm April weekends he seemed to choose the bumpiest, most untended roads. She would always need to find a bathroom. At first this amused him, but soon his amusement became sardonic. He pulled in at gas stations where he didn't need gas and waited in the car with folded arms and a sullen expression that made her apologetic. They were growing apart again, fading away from each other. She could feel the distance between them once more like a patch of fog, dimming and distorting the relations of curves in space. The baby that lay between them in the dark was pushing them apart.

Sometimes as she lay awake at night Caroline brooded over the deformities the baby might be born with: clubfoot, arms like fins, two heads. She wondered if she could love a baby with a gross defect. She wondered if Ivan would want to put it in an institution, and if there were any decent places nearby, and if they would be spending every Sunday afternoon for the rest of their lives visiting the baby and driving home heartbroken in silence. She lived through these visits to the institution in vivid detail till she knew the doctors' and nurses' faces well. There would come a point in her fantasies when Ivan, selfish with his time and impatient with futility, would refuse to go any more, and she would have to go alone. She wondered if Ivan ever thought about these things, but with that cold mood of his she was afraid to ask.

One night she couldn't bear the heaviness any longer so she woke him. "Ivan. I'm so lonely."

He sat up abruptly. "What?" With the dark hair hanging down over his stunned face he looked boyish and vulnerable. She felt sorry for him.

"I know you were sleeping but I—I just lie here forever in the dark and think awful things and you're so far away, I can't stand it."

"Oh, Caroline. Oh, baby." Now he was wide awake, and took her in his arms. "I know. I know it's hard for you. You're so—everything is so different, that's all."

"But, Ivan, it's still me."

"I know it's stupid of me. I can't—"

She knew what it was. It would never be the same. They sat up all night holding each other, and talking. Ivan talked more than he had in weeks. He said the baby would be perfectly all right and it would be born at the right time too, late June, so she could finish up the term, and they would start their natural childbirth class in two weeks so he could be with her and help her, though of course she would do it easily because she was so competent at everything. Then they would have the summer for the early difficult months, and she would be feeling fine and be ready to go back to work in the fall. They would find a good person, someone like a grandmother, to come in, and he would try to stagger his schedule so she would not feel overburdened and trapped. In short, everything would be just fine, and they would make love again like they used to and be close again. He said exactly what she needed to hear, while she huddled against him wrenched with pain because he had known all along the right words to say but hadn't thought to say them till she woke him in despair. Still, in the dawn she slept contented. She loved him; it was a tropism.

They went to the opening of a show by a group of young local artists. Ivan had helped them get a grant and was to be publicly thanked at a dinner. Caroline, near the end of her eighth month, walked around for an hour looking at paintings and refusing the glasses of champagne thrust at her, then whispered to Ivan, "Listen, I'm sorry but I've got to go. Give me the car keys, will you? I don't feel up to it."

"What's the matter?"

"My feet are killing me, my head aches, and the kid is rolling around like a basketball. You stay and enjoy it. You can get a ride with someone. I'll see you later."

"I'll drive you home," he said grimly. "We'll leave."

An awful knot gripped her stomach. The knot was the image of his perverse resistance, the immense trouble coming, all the troubles they had ever had congealed and tied up in one moment. They smiled at passers-by while they whispered ferociously to each other.

"Ivan, I do not want you to take me home. This is your event. Stay. I am leaving. We are separate people."

"If you feel that bad you can't drive home alone. You're my wife and I'll take you home."

"Suit yourself," she said sweetly, because the director of the gallery was approaching. "We both know you're much bigger and stronger than I am. You've proven that already." And she smiled maliciously.

Ivan waved vaguely at the director and ushered her to the door. Outside he exploded.

"Shit, Caroline! We can't do a fucking thing any more, can we?"

"You can do anything you please, as always. All you have to do is give me the keys. I left mine home."

"Get in the car. You're supposed to be feeling sick."

"You big resentful selfish idiot. Jealous of an embryo!" She was screaming now. He started the car with a rush that jolted her forward against the dashboard. "I'd be better off driving myself. You'll kill me this way."

"Shut the hell up or I swear I'll go into a tree," he shouted. "I don't give a shit any more."

It was starting to rain, a soft silent rain that glittered in the drab dusk outside. At exactly the same moment they rolled up their windows. They were sealed in together, she thought, like restless beasts in a cage. Like the wolf beneath the magnificent piazza. The air in the car was dank and stuffy.

When they got home he slammed the door so hard the house shook. Caroline had calmed herself. She sank down in a chair and kicked off her shoes. "Ivan, why don't you go back? It's not too late. These dinners are always late anyway. I'll be okay."

"I don't want to go back," he yelled. "The whole thing is spoiled. Our whole lives are spoiled from now on. We were better off before. I thought you had gotten over wanting it. I thought it was a dead issue." He stared at her bulging stomach with such loathing that she was shocked into lucid perception.

"You disgust me," she said quietly. "Frankly, you always have and probably always will." She didn't know why she said that. It was quite untrue. It was only true that he disgusted her at this moment, yet the rest had rolled out like string from a hidden ball of twine.

"So why did we ever start this in the first place?" he screamed.

She didn't know whether he meant the marriage or the baby, and for an instant she thought he might hit her, there was such compressed force in his shoulders.

"Get the hell out of here, Ivan. I don't want to have to look at you."

"I will. I'll go back. I'll take your advice. Call your fucking obstetrician if you need anything. I'm sure he's always glad of an extra feel."

"You ignorant pig. Go on. And don't hurry back. Find yourself a skinny little art student and give her a big treat."

"I just might." He slammed the door and the house shook again.

He would be back. Only this time she felt no secret excitement, no tremor that could reshape into passion; she was too burdened down. The ugly words would lie between them like a dead weight till weeks after the baby was born, till Ivan felt he had reclaimed his rightful territory. Caroline took two aspirins. When she woke at three he was in bed beside her, gripping the blanket in his sleep and breathing heavily. For days afterwards they spoke with strained, sub-dued courtesy.

They worked diligently in the natural childbirth classes once a week, while at home they giggled over how silly the exercises were. Ivan insisted she pant her five minutes each day as instructed. As relaxation training, Ivan was sup-posed to lift each of her legs and arms three times and drop them, while she lay perfectly limp and passive. From the start Caroline was excellent at this routine, which they did in bed before going to sleep. A substitute, she thought. She could make her body so limp and passive that her arms and legs bounced when they fell. One night for diversion she tried doing it to him.

"Don't do anything, Ivan. I lift the leg and I drop the leg. Surrender. Then you can have a baby too."

But he couldn't master the technique of passivity. He tried to be limp, but she could see his muscles, precisely those leg muscles she found so alluring, exerting to lift and drop, lift and drop.

"You can't give yourself up." She laughed. "Don't you feel what you're doing? Lie still and let me do it to you."

"Oh, forget it, Caroline." He smiled up at her and stroked her stomach gently. "What's the difference? I don't have to do it well. You do it very well."

She did it very well indeed when the time came. It was an extremely short labor, very unusual for a first baby, the nurses kept muttering. She breathed intently, beginning with the long slow breaths she had been taught, feeling remote from the bustle around her. Then in a flurry they raced her down the hall on a wheeled table with a pack of white-coated people trotting after, and she thought, panting, No matter what I suffer, soon I will be thin again.

The room was crowded with people, far more people than she would have thought necessary, but the only faces she singled out were Ivan's and the doctor's. The doctor, plump and framed by her knees, was wildly enthusiastic about the proceedings. "Terrific, Caroline, terrific," he yelled cheerfully, as if they were in a noisy sports arena. "Okay, start pushing."

They placed her hands on chrome rails along the table. On the left, groping, she found Ivan's hand and held it instead of the rail. She pushed. In astonishment she became aware of a great cleavage, like a mountain of granite splitting apart, only it was in her, and if it kept on going it would go right up to her neck. She gripped Ivan's warm hand. Just as she opened her mouth to roar someone clapped an oxygen mask on her face so the roar reverberated inward on her own ears. She wasn't supposed to roar, the natural childbirth teacher hadn't mentioned anything about that, she was supposed to breathe and push. But as long as no one seemed to take any notice she might as well keep on, it felt so satisfying and necessary. The teacher would never know. The sound reminded her of something she had heard long ago, but she was so caught up in the pushing she couldn't remember what. She trusted that if she split all the way up to her neck they would sew her up somehow— she was too far gone to worry about that now. Maybe that was why there were so many of them, yes, of course, to put her back together, and maybe they had simply forgotten to tell her about being bisected; or maybe it was a closely guarded secret, like an initiation rite. She gripped Ivan's hand tighter. She was not having too terrible a time, she would surely survive, she told herself, captivated by the hellish wolf-like sounds going from her mouth to her ear; it was what her students would call a peak experience, and how gratifying to hear the doctor exclaim, "Oh, this is one terrific girl! One more, Caroline, give me one more push and send it out. Sock it to me."

She raised herself on her elbows, and staring straight at him, gave him with tremendous force the final push he asked for. She had Ivan's hand tightly around the rail, could feel his knuckles bursting, and then all of a sudden the room and the faces disappeared. A dark thick curtain wrapped swiftly around her and she was left all alone gasping, sucked violently into a windy black hole of pain so explosive she knew it must be death, she was dying fast, like a bomb detonating. It was all right, it was almost over, she was almost dead, only she would have liked to see those flawed green eyes one last time.

From somewhere in the void Ivan's voice shouted in exultation, "It's coming out," and then the roaring stopped and there was peace and quiet in her ears. The curtain fell away, the world returned. But her eyes kept on burning, as if they had seen something not meant for living eyes to see and return from alive.

"Give it to me," Caroline said, and held it. She saw that every part was in the proper place, and shut her eyes.

They wheeled her to a room and eased her onto the bed. It was past ten in the morning. She dimly remembered they had been up all night watching a James Cagney movie about prize-fighting while they timed her irregular mild contractions. James Cagney went blind from blows given by poisoned gloves in a rigged match, and she wept for him as she held her hands on her stomach and breathed. Neither she nor Ivan had slept or eaten for hours.

"Ivan, there is something I am really dying to have right this minute."

"Your wish is my command."

She wanted roast beef on rye with ketchup, and iced tea.

He brought it and stood at the window while she ate rave-
nously.

"Didn't you get anything for yourself?"

"No, I'm too exhausted to eat." He did look terrible.
He was sallow; his eyes, usually so radiant, were nearly
drained of color, and small downward-curving lines around
his mouth recalled his laborious vigil.

"You had a rough night, Ivan. You ought to get some
sleep. What's it like outside?"

"What?" Ivan's movements seemed purposeless. He was
pacing the room with his hands deep in his pockets, going
slowly from the foot of the bed to the window and back.
Every now and then he stopped to peer at Caroline in an
unfamiliar way, as if she were a puzzling stranger.

"Ivan, are you okay? I meant the weather. What's it doing
outside?" It struck her, as she asked, that it was weeks since
she had cared to know anything about the outside. That
there was an outside, now that she was emptied out, came
rushing at her with the most urgent importance, wafting
her on a tide of grateful joy.

"Oh," he said vaguely, and came to sit on the edge of
her bed. "Well, it's doing something very peculiar outside,
as a matter of fact. It's raining but the sun is shining."

She laughed. "Haven't you ever seen it do that before?"

"I don't know. I guess so." He opened his mouth and
closed it several times. She waited, eating her sandwich.
At last he spoke. "You know, Caroline, you really have
quite a grip. When you were holding my hand in there,
you squeezed it so tight I thought you would break it."

"Oh, come on, that can't be."

"I'm not joking." He massaged his hand absently, then
held it out and showed her the raw red knuckles and palm,
with raised flaming welts forming.

She took his hand. "You're serious. Did I do that? Well,

how do you like that? I finally won a round."

"I really thought you'd break my hand. It was killing me." He repeated it, not resentfully but dully, as though there were something secreted in the words that he couldn't fathom.

"But why didn't you take it away if it hurt that badly?" She put down her half-eaten sandwich as she saw the pale amazement ripple over his face.

"Oh no, I couldn't do that. I mean—if that was what you needed just then—" He looked away, embarrassed. "We're in a hospital, after all." He shrugged, not facing her. "What better place? They'd fix it for me."

Overwhelmed, Caroline lay back on the pillows. "Oh, Ivan. You would do that?"

"What are you crying for?" he asked gently. "You didn't break it, did you? Almost doesn't count. So what are you crying about? You just had a baby. Don't cry."

And she smiled and thought her heart would burst.

The baby was Isabel, an almost perfect baby. At birth she resembled her father, dark, long, and lean, and she remained so through the years of her childhood. Caroline and Ivan welcomed her with bemused surprise like an unexpected treasure, a windfall, so that she grew happily. It was natural to treat her like a treasure because she was so agreeable, as if upon joining their family—creating for them a family— she had pledged not to be disruptive, to do her necessary crying and falling and experience her necessary frustrations with the least disturbance. She was readily soothed. Nor did goodness make her bland. Her father's daughter, she was a child of wit and energy and grace, who spoke, as an only child does, with a winning fluency. Envious friends warned that such children become terrible in adolescence, saving up, as it were, the powers of destruction, but Caroline and Ivan, restored to grateful calm after years of agitation, lived in the present. They had an elderly baby-sitter who took care of her during the days so Caroline could teach, but she dropped whatever administrative tasks she could, and did fewer projects of her own. Ivan became a true father as he had promised so long ago: not only did he tend and nurture, but he woke for night feedings, he diapered, he pushed the stroller.

He was always glad, that first year, to get her alone. Filled with relief that her shape had re-emerged after the pregnancy, he pursued her greedily, reminding her of the high school boys whose hands had ceaselessly and involuntarily twitched and roamed. She would laugh to herself when she came downstairs after putting the baby to bed and read the jittery message in his eyes. Working and caring for Isabel, she was tired, and often she couldn't fully savor his passion. But she was happy to know it existed, still, because of her. She was happy in his arms. When he told her she was growing passive she tried to be more active. It didn't strike her as too important either way, active or passive, she was so relieved herself to have finished with pregnancy and childbirth.

And then, when the baby began to sleep and eat on a civilized schedule and amuse herself for spells during the day, Caroline's passion returned. Ivan's cooled. Isabel was more of an intriguing presence now. She was delighted to greet her father at the door each night. Ivan saw his face mirrored in hers. He whispered words to her that Caroline couldn't hear, he took her for walks alone at twilight on the shady green streets and returned proudly bearing anecdotes of her wit. It was Caroline, more often now, who pursued with a glittering eye. But she hardly worried; she understood it was rare for lovers' cycles to coincide. He would be back.

Isabel had just one noticeable flaw, and that was a right eye that did not focus properly. It turned in. The doctor said to operate, the sooner the better. She was four. Caroline spent the night before the operation tossing on a cot alongside Isabel's hospital bed, getting up intermittently to watch snatches of old movies on television in the patients' lounge. Ivan came the next morning, barely in time to say hello and good-bye to Isabel as a young bearded attendant strapped her to a wheeled table. She was holding a stuffed replica of Babar the elephant and seemed inordinately cheerful, far more interested in the handsome green-coated attendant than in Ivan. They gazed after as the attendant wheeled her, much too quickly, Caroline felt, to the doors of the elevator. He jiggled the table in time to a Beatles tune he was singing to Isabel.

"You're wearing your glasses," said Caroline.

"My eyes were burning."

A passing nurse suggested they might want to go to the staff cafeteria, since it would be a long wait.

"How long?" asked Ivan.

"Two hours. Maybe more. We'll let you know as soon as she's in the recovery room."

At the words "recovery room," Caroline's heart leaped to her throat. Her father had gone to the recovery room but never recovered. Now Isabel was her only blood kin.

The staff cafeteria, at the end of a series of musty tiled basement corridors, was filled with young men and women in white uniforms, chattering and laughing.

"Do you mean to say these are doctors?" asked Caroline.

"They must be students. Anyway, they're down here, not up there. Look, Caroline, you get a table and sit down. You look terrible. What do you want to eat?"

"Coffee, black, with something. Anything."

He brought two coffees and two pecan danishes with coconut sprinkled on top. His hands trembled when he set down the mugs. After eleven years of marriage, she thought, coconut. She hated coconut, but she bit into it.

"Isn't it strange that we can sit here and eat while our child is being cut up?" she said.

"Don't you remember what that lady in Rome told us? You have to eat no matter what happens. Wars, assassinations, minor surgery. Just keep eating."

"Maybe I'll have another, then." It was amazing how, since her pregnancy, she had never had any more stomach trouble. She had developed what Ivan's father called a cast-iron stomach. They must remember to call Ivan's parents later, to let them know everything was all right.

Ivan started to get up.

"No, it's okay. I'll go this time. How about you?"

"Oh, all right, bring me a roll and some scrambled eggs and bacon, and more coffee."

She found a pastry without coconut. After they ate, Ivan took a deck of cards out of his pocket.

"Do you want to play gin?"

"When you play with me, it's not even a challenge."

"You have a chance," he said. "I'm not in my best form. Anyway, you have the basic ability. Your problem is that you don't concentrate."

"Thank you, Jerome."

They went up to the main floor to play. The waiting room was enormous, with deep brown leather seats and huge teardrop chandeliers. The few people scattered about were reading newspapers. War was raging. Students were demonstrating. Ivan shuffled the cards and they cascaded to the floor. "I guess I'm nervous," he said, picking them up. "Did I ever tell you that I had an operation like this when I was a kid?"

"No, you never told me," she said. "How come you don't tell me these things?"

"I was seven."

"Well, how did it feel?"

"It wasn't bad."

She looked up and hesitated. "They didn't fix it exactly right."

"I know, but it came out much better than it was. They did the best they could. They've improved the technique a lot over the years."

"We'll soon see."

Ivan won four games handily. He put the cards back in his pocket and got up to pace the room. When he returned he said, "Caroline?"

"What?"

"Are you glad we met?"

She didn't want to be bothered. She was sewing, and she wanted to be lost in her cross-stitches. They were very absorbing, very soothing in their unvarying monotony. She had never seen Ivan so fidgety. "What a question."

"Are you? I mean—" and he smiled weakly—"with my defective eye genes and all?"

"You're not so defective. You're all right."

She wore glasses herself now, for close work. She adjusted them and bent over her sewing.

"What's that thing you're doing?"

"It's a sampler, to embroider. I bought it in the gift shop yesterday."

"You mean one of those things that says God Bless Our Happy Home? Let me see."

She held it up. "No, see, this one just has the alphabet, in big and small letters, and flowers."

"I never saw you do embroidery before. Since when is this?"

"I sew on special occasions. I've already done the capital X and the J, and the small a,d, and f, and two roses, and I'm working on the q."

He gave her an odd look. "Well, I think I'll go and ask at the desk."

"It's only an hour and a quarter."

"I'll ask anyway." He returned in a moment, unsatisfied, and sat down. "Oh, I forgot to tell you the good news. We had a letter from Vic yesterday. He's getting married."

Caroline put down the embroidery and took off her glasses. "Vic is? That's wonderful! Who's he marrying?" Vic was thirty-five, the same age as she was. His single state had been preoccupying Ivan's parents for years.

"Someone named Susan. She's a lawyer too. She works

in his office. They're going to move to New York and set up a practice, so we'll get to see them more often. In fact, they're having the wedding in New York in a couple of months, so we can go."

If she lives, thought Caroline, we'll go. "That's wonderful, Ivan. I'm really glad. Did he say how come this one, after all the others?"

"I suppose Miss Right just came along. Or Ms. Right, I should say."

"Oh, Miss Right. You always said you didn't believe in Miss Right. You said everything was random. Like us."

"They're not necessarily mutually exclusive."

She pondered that for a few seconds, then said dryly, "I'm deeply touched," and resumed sewing.

Ivan inquired at the desk about Isabel three times and was embarrassed to ask again. "You go this time, Caroline."

"You were just there a minute ago. I don't like the way that woman looks. She'll yell at me, and I don't feel like being yelled at."

"Please."

The woman, who had a greenish pallor, fixed bulging eyes on Caroline and tightened her lips. "I have already told your husband you would be informed," she said, and turned her back.

"Oh, fuck off," said Caroline under her breath. A young man typing behind the desk caught her eye and grinned.

They were summoned five minutes later. "The child is in the recovery room," the frog-faced woman said.

"But when can we see her?"

"You may go up to her room now. They'll be bringing her back shortly."

Caroline turned from the desk and fell weeping into Ivan's arms. "I was so scared. Oh God, I was so scared. This was much worse than having her."

"It's all right now, baby. Everything's all right. It was nothing, a small thing."

"I am glad we met, Ivan. I am."

Isabel was given a pair of dark glasses with round lenses and pink plastic frames, and told to wear them outdoors for two days. In front of the hospital, Caroline dropped the sampler in a wastebasket and studied her. Her heart quickened: with the glasses, Isabel looked like a blind person. But they would be home soon and she could take them off. She herself could hardly wait to get to bed—she hadn't slept for two nights.

"These are good glasses," said Isabel. "I'm going to wear them to school."

Ivan said, "Maybe we should get her a box of pencils."

"Ivan, really." But she laughed.

"I don't want pencils," said Isabel. "I want my sandals."

Ivan looked down at her feet, in plaid sneakers. "What sandals?"

"Mommy promised if I didn't scream when they took my blood I could get sandals after. I didn't scream."

"We'll get them tomorrow."

"You said as soon as it was over," said Isabel pleasantly. "Don't you remember?"

Ivan was opening the car door. Caroline looked over at him. "Please stop at a shoe store," she said. "I did promise. There must be something nearby."

"I saw the kind I want at Jack and Jill."

At night they fell asleep instantly. Caroline awoke to the particular stillness of the hour before first light. She relived her stay in the hospital, the television vigils, the hard cot, the babies with gross deformities and their hapless mothers. The singing attendant, the coconut danish, Ivan dropping the cards. When she had run it through she had the blessed relief of waking from a nightmare. All was well. The stillness around her deepened, and in the dark hour descended like a visitation of grace one of those moments when miraculously it is clear that all things will be well. She knew by now how ephemeral such moments were, and how they must be savored. Except that Ivan, in his sleep, began groping around her back and hips. She was used to his restless sleep, less sleep than a muted form of action. He liked to cling to her at night, as a displaced person journeying to parts unknown clings to a loved relic of home. She didn't mind; it made her feel needed. But this was extreme: he fumbled in blind frustration with the light fabric of her nightgown. Not for love; had he wanted that he would have whispered her name and groped in a way more calculated to arouse. He was fast asleep, tugging and pulling. All at once in the clarity of the darkness she understood. What he wanted was a feeling. What he wanted, after his own nightmare, was to touch living skin. She was awed by the rareness of him, a creature of such unimpeded instinct that even in sleep he sought what he needed. As she raised the nightgown for him his hands settled on her skin and he quieted, breathing evenly.

It was by accident, a few months later, that she heard Ivan talking about the sense of touch. Vic and his wife, Susan, were up for a long weekend. Susan was Miss Right, Ivan and Caroline agreed. She and Vic were alike—hearty, gregarious, and clever. They even looked alike, both sturdy with ruddy outdoor faces, neatly combed hair and frank brown eyes, the muscled right arms of tennis players. Their life in New York was busy and sociable, and they seemed surprised, in a benign way, that Caroline and Ivan could find enough stimulation in a small university town. They held hands on the couch as they sipped their wine. If one of them needed a hand to light a cigarette or put cheese on a cracker, the hand was reluctantly withdrawn and quickly returned. "Disgusting," Caroline and Ivan joked in private, in bed, playing their rough games of hide-and-seek with hands. Vic and Susan called each other sweetheart and darling all the time, which she and Ivan laughed at too, benignly, in private. They were planning to start a family right away, Susan said, since they were not getting any younger.

Caroline put Isabel to bed and got out another bottle of wine. Just as she came into the room Ivan was saying, "But still, the senses exist in very different proportions in different people." He sat in the rocking chair with the fingertips of both hands gently tapping against each other. "I don't hear a lot, for example—I mean the fine gradations that some people do. That Caroline does. With me it's the sense of touch. I guess I come to know things by touching them." He paused a moment, letting each fingertip meet its opposite one in turn, like playing a silent scale on the piano. "I like to feel the textures of things."

She set down the wine very quietly. It was so intimate, especially coming from Ivan. More intimate, somehow, than revealing a visual or auditory bent. Vic and Susan regarded him curiously.

Susan said that that was more or less what she meant in the first place, that Ivan was as different from Vic as brothers could be. Vic was so intellectual; she was always telling him he should get more in touch with his feelings.

"But I wasn't talking about any pop psychology," said Ivan kindly. "I was talking about primary, sensory experience. Before the emotions, even."

Touch was the most primitive. In all their years together he had never told her that.

She lay in bed waiting for him while he brushed his hair, examining it in front of the mirror as he did nightly, for signs of thinning. There came a rhythmic rustling from the next room, where Vic and Susan were staying.

"They're starting a family," said Caroline.

"And getting in touch with their feelings," said Ivan.

"Oh, talking about feelings, you never told me about your sense of touch. . . . Sweetheart."

"No?"

"No. That's very important."

"I never thought of it. I suppose I thought you knew."

Of course, she did know. The hands on her skin at night, coming to know her by the touch. Except she needed to hear him speak it aloud to know that she knew.

Ivan approached her earnestly, brush in hand. "Caroline? I mean, darling, do you think my hair is getting any thinner? Feel."

"It feels fine. I can't feel any difference."

He squinted at her. "I think you're just being kind."

"You know I'm not kind that way. I'd tell you the truth. Oh, all right, just a few hairs less. Nothing to worry about. You're still beautiful."

"That is not an objective opinion," he said.

"I can't help it. I do my best. Listen, Ivan." She put her hand on his. "Do you really think I ought to go, this winter? You give me an objective opinion."

"My opinion is yes, you should definitely go. Why all the fuss?"

She had been invited to spend three months—a trimester—as a visiting professor at a small college in the north woods, giving advanced seminars in topological groups and the topology of manifolds.

"Go ahead. You'll be on loan," her department head quipped when she showed him the letter. "We'll manage." He sounded like Ivan.

She was hesitant about leaving Isabel, who was five, but Ivan kept reassuring her that everything would be all right. Mrs. Seward would pick her up at nursery school and stay in the afternoons.

"But she can't stay long enough to cook dinner."

"I'll cook."

"You'll cook! But your cooking is too fancy for her." In cooking he lacked the common touch. His hamburgers were leaden, fortified with bread crumbs. The first evening he had asked her to his apartment in Rome he let the chicken burn to a crisp while he described how the lights on the Ponte Vecchio were reflected in the Arno on a summer night. The description made her shiver with love, yet she felt he should have been able to manage lyricism and chicken at the same time.

"I'll make Chinese food," he said. "She likes that. Don't worry about it." It was true, he did quite well with Chinese food. He had taken a course.

He urged her on, countering all her doubts with reason. At night, lying close in bed, she teased him, running a finger vertically down the hairs of his chest. "Why are you so eager for me to go?"

"Because it will be good for you," he answered seriously. She felt a stirring of love. But hours later she awoke and heard those words resound in the dark air. Were they patronizing words, perhaps?

Patronizing or not, they were correct, and she would go. She was excited by the change, and by the prospect of the seminars, new colleagues with new ideas, and solitary walks in the snowy north woods. In her life now she missed solitude. She wondered what she would be like in solitude, what her habits would be, if she would enjoy her own company or be bored.

The first few weeks in the north woods she was very happy. The classes went well, the students were bright, and the other teachers congenial. She had a small, pleasant efficiency apartment in a low building housing some twenty single faculty members. Her private office was luxurious compared to the one she shared at her own university, and it looked out over a vista of imposing evergreens in precise, satisfying rows. Best of all were the long walks in the woods along cleared snowy trails. Caroline shook the laden branches of trees and laughed as heaps of snow came tumbling down around her and over her. She discovered small bubbling waterfalls that trickled into lively ripples edging the frozen surfaces of ponds. There was even a romantic old stone tower on a hill. She clambered up with the exaltation of a prince going to rescue a maiden from captivity. She was not bored; she found herself excellent company. In the evenings she sometimes ate alone in her apartment with a book propped on the table, and sometimes, if she felt like talk, in the faculty dining room. Late at night she read Proust in bed, and smoked.

At the beginning her mind would stop abruptly at odd moments like a train pulling up short, and she would think: Where is Isabel now? Isabel is at nursery school, listening to a story. Isabel is in the bathtub with her rubber fish. Isabel is having dinner. (What bizarre Asiatic concoction is she eating? Has he taught her to use chopsticks?) But in time those questions stopped. Caroline wrote Isabel letters and received in return stick-figure drawings with a few tender penciled words slanting downward across the page. These she treasured.

She spoke to Ivan occasionally on the telephone, late at night. The first few times she hung up feeling weak-kneed with want, from the sound of his voice. Soon she began to long, uncomfortably, for someone to make love to her. She gaped childishly at any chance muscled body glimpsed in the drugstore or the bank. Reading the lush rhythmic prose of Proust aroused her. The homosexual and the sadistic passages aroused her most. She worried briefly about the possible implications of this, then decided there were none, she simply needed someone. Tentatively, she took a look around.

Her department, mathematics, consisted of an elderly patriarch, a tired married man in his mid-fifties, and a chubby precocious boy of twenty-five, whom she thought of as The Callow Youth. The English department occurred to her. English departments were generally large, and their members reputed to be forever in quest of sensation. She assumed it came from dwelling so continuously in poems and stories. Gazing in the mirror at her unappreciated body, she was embarrassed to acknowledge her undertaking. But surely she was a grown woman now, she retorted to the image, old enough to know what she needed and seek means to obtain it. Hadn't Ivan once said she looked like the kind who could go after what she wanted? And this was another world—no one who mattered would ever know.

She began eating in the faculty dining room more frequently and more attentively. Of the English department's three single men, one was a perpetually disgruntled Australian poet with rotting teeth, and another a specialist in Middle English, whose flailing morning hesitancy suggested that he drank all night. The last, a recent arrival, taught Victorian and modern poetry and dressed in neat faded jeans and cashmere sweaters in rich colors—wine, olive, sienna. Tall, fair-skinned, and mustached, he wore aviator-style tinted glasses, the same as hers. Common tastes. He seemed about her age too, perhaps a few years younger—old enough, anyway, to have had some experience. He had an incipient pot belly, which she would have to learn to ignore, but otherwise he was well-built, with long legs and tight muscles, and he moved easily, with comfortable nonchalance. Only his voice made her hesitate: it was strained, as if from inner tension withheld. Yet he could laugh readily at a joke with a disarmingly modest, amused light in his blue eyes. She had an old unsatisfied hunger for blue eyes, ever since the editor of the high school paper who put his hand under her skirt on her mother's couch. His name was John and he was shy. It would take some doing.

She first engaged his interest over the Ping-Pong table in the lounge of the faculty dining room. They played similarly: with fervor, their pride at stake in every volley, castigating themselves for errors and relishing a point well taken. Neither of them was often able to outplay the other—the mistakes were mostly self-destructive. He told her that a point lost in that fashion was called an "unforced error." Caroline marveled at the ramifications of that term, unforced error, but John did not seem to appreciate its nuances, as Ivan would have.

After a few nights they grew adapted to each other's style and developed canny modes of retaliation. He had an angled, menacing serve; Caroline learned to stand near the right-hand corner of the table, to return it. Her plays were swift, if erratic; he learned to adjust his timing. More and more they indulged in prolonged, deceptively relaxed volleys, playing a waiting game, alert for the other's slip in attention. She felt with him, during those passages, the tacit intimacy of opponents, really accomplices secretly finding and inhabiting each other's rhythm. The long volleys usually ended with his slamming the ball hard in a burst of violence: these were either brilliant strokes, irretrievable, or else they veered absurdly, bouncing off the walls and ceiling. She laughed out loud at his unlikely recklessness. Yes, she decided after many evenings of Ping-Pong and careful scrutiny, that is the man.

The first time they made love she responded to him with

the stored desire of five weeks. He will believe that I am mad about him, she thought; he will not understand that it is desperation. But then it hardly mattered.

She was right. John, who even in intimacy kept a vestige of shyness, was pleased and flattered. Without his glasses his eyes were a richer blue, and they glowed with an appealing, gentle pride. Leaning over her, his fair hair brushing her face, he smiled with a tremulous curve of the lips she had never seen across the Ping-Pong table. An amused twinkle sprang to his eyes as he said, "If you like that so much I'll be glad to do it again sometime."

He was a very lovable man, she realized with some surprise.

"Oh, by all means."

Not bad, she congratulated herself, not bad for a small out-of-the-way college in the north woods.

One evening Ivan said over the phone, "I'm so busy here that in the whole time you've been gone I've only read forty pages of *The Dream of the Red Chamber.*" He made it sound tragic.

"I'm sorry." I've read three volumes of Proust, she added silently, with guilt.

"Things are awful at work. Lanier quit without any notice and left a six-month backlog of stuff not done. It took us three days just to go through it."

"Oh, Lord!"

"There's so much laundry. And Isabel has started staying up so late at night."

"How late?"

"Nine. Nine-thirty."

"Well, why don't you make her go to bed?"

"I don't know, it's kind of nice having her around. It's so quiet in the evenings."

"Well—"

"I'm not complaining."

"You're certainly giving a good imitation."

"How are you? How is it going out there?"

"Fine. Really fine." She had no desire to tell him much over the phone. She would tell him when she got back. Ivan seemed very remote now, while John was close to hand, palpable. It made her happy to have John around, even though she did not love him. He didn't break in on her solitude the way Ivan did, nor did she need to think about him when he was not with her. Sometimes even when he was, she thought about events in her past, or her work, or the volume of Proust she was up to, things that had nothing to do with him and that she had no wish to share. Her walks in the snow were not spoiled by his company. He was a hand to hold, someone to show her discoveries— the waterfalls, the tower—yet they remained no less hers. Ivan would have infiltrated the north woods. At home he infiltrated everywhere. The air around him carried a magnetic charge that distorted her sense of boundaries. There was no solitude.

She and John, meanwhile, discovered that beyond sex, they had enough to talk about: New England, where they had both grown up; music, which Ivan knew nothing about; politics—John didn't think anarchism was so impracticable; painting. What she knew about painting she knew from Ivan, she remembered guiltily whenever she said something intelligent. They also liked to play chess, which Ivan hated because he lost to her, eat pizza, throw snowballs at each other, and do all the things that lovers do. But we are not really lovers, Caroline thought. She hoped John did not love her. He had never said so. She did not want to leave wrenching pain behind her when she left; her own memories would be pain enough. And she was only on loan, after all.

In another telephone conversation Ivan said, "Isabel's

been invited to a birthday party, a new boy in her class, Dick, but she doesn't want to go."

"Why not?"

"She says she doesn't like him."

"Why doesn't she like him?"

"Well, listen to this, this is terrific. She has three reasons for not liking him. He's too fat, he spits when he talks, and his shirt hangs out over his pants."

Caroline laughed.

"I tried to tell her those are no reasons to condemn a person, but she really is set against going."

"I don't blame her. I think those are pretty good reasons for not liking a person."

"Oh, Caroline, really. My shirts sometimes hang out."

"But you don't spit," she said.

"Oh no? I'm going to spit right now. Watch out." He made a succulent sound into the phone.

Suddenly he was not remote at all. He had infiltrated the north woods. She slumped back in her chair. "I miss you," she whispered.

"I miss you too. I put your pillows away. There were too many on the bed. Four. They made me lonely so I put your two in the closet."

"Oh, Ivan, how could you?"

"The sheets are cold," he said.

"Please."

The next evening, with John, she felt something she recognized in panic was very like love. She clung to him and asked him to stay the night. She had never wanted that before. She felt a pang of delayed jealousy over the woman he had been married to for three years, a decade ago. What kind of woman would John choose as a wife? While he slept she spent a long time staring at him, and traced the lines of his face, neck and shoulder with her finger, very lightly so he wouldn't wake. She wondered if she was headed for trouble.

But that passed, and then for the first time she knew a shallow duplicity, for all along she had felt her integrity rested in keeping John and Ivan distinct.

When it was time to leave she packed her bags with eagerness. John drove her to the train in the pale early morning light. Weeks ago she had imagined herself thanking him kindly for the many hours of good company, but when the moment came she could not summon such detachment. He had become too real.

"I hope you're not going to be very unhappy," she said. "You knew it was just for a little while." She heard her words as callous, and saw herself as a character in the kind of 1940s movie she and Ivan liked to watch late at night on television, a male character, Charles Boyer or Humphrey Bogart with important secret missions, not the type to be relied on for permanent arrangements. It was not a pleasant image.

"I knew," John said. His blue eyes shone behind the aviator glasses with an odd light she hoped was not tears. "You will write, though, won't you?"

"Of course," said Caroline, and she left the north woods.

All day, on the train and in the first hours at home, admiring Isabel's stack of abstract paintings from nursery school, resettling things on her desk and in her closet, checking to see what Oriental oddments were in the refrigerator, John was a shadow over her shoulder. But at night when Ivan touched her the shadow vanished. He made everything vanish.

"Let me see if you still feel the same," he said.

"I'm so glad to be home," Caroline said as she embraced him. In a while, amidst pleasure, she had a fleeting image of John at the train station gallantly holding her bags, with possible tears in his eyes.

"Well, tell me, do I feel any different?"

"Yes," he said.

She moved from him, surprised. "How?"

He touched her like a blind man. "You feel as if you've been somewhere else."

"I have been somewhere else. What do you mean?"

Ivan was silent.

"What are you not saying? Say it."

"No. So long as you came back."

"Well, of course."

In the morning she awoke to the sound of soft voices behind her. She could feel Isabel's hand resting on the curve of her hip.

"His name is Koh Ma. I don't like him. He goes around hitting everyone in the class."

"Have you told him to stop?" Ivan asked.

"I tell him, but he doesn't understand. He can't talk. He only talks Chinese."

"Korean, I think it is."

"There was this doll, and he grabbed it and said 'dog.'"

"He's learning English. Why don't you try teaching him some words?"

"I don't like people who hit. I don't hit. More of the boys hit. When you were younger did you use to hit girls?"

Ivan gave a deep sigh. "Talk softly. Mommy's here now, remember? She's still sleeping."

"Well, did you?" Isabel whispered. "Hit girls?"

"Everybody does things, when they're very angry, that they're sorry for later. But sometimes they can't help it."

"But did *you?*"

"Well, to be honest, I suppose I did." He paused for a moment. "Once or twice."

"You don't hit me."

"That's different. This boy, Koh Ma—he hits because he's frustrated. I mean, he can't show what he wants any other way. Probably once he learns to speak English he'll stop hitting."

"Whenever we sing a song he yells."

"How do you think you would feel if you were in his country and all the kids were singing something you couldn't understand?"

"I wouldn't yell."

Ivan laughed. "Don't be too sure, sweetheart."

Caroline turned around. Isabel, wearing the dark glasses she had saved from last year's operation, was sitting up in the center of the bed facing Ivan. As she talked his hand stroked her sleek dark head from the wide forehead back down the sweep of smooth hair, in long slow strokes. His hand covered almost her whole head. He didn't notice that Caroline was awake: he was staring at the child, absorbed in the touch, burying his fingers in her fine hair while she chattered on. They were quite content without her, she thought. All the time she was gone they had lived like this, happily ever after, a fairy tale's sequel. Her feeling for John was nothing like this. An unease woke in her blood and spread through her every cell.

When she remarked, much later, that he loved the child more than he loved her he denied it, naturally. He said he loved Isabel not more but differently. "Can't you see that? It's so obvious. It's a different kind of relationship." It was jarring to hear Ivan use words like "relationship"; it made her doubt certain coveted visions she still had of him: that he was the noble savage who had approached her warily, with subtle grace, through the crowd. Or else the reverse, self-made eighteenth-century man released from

the Augustan setting—balanced and serene, witty and senti-
mental, yet more attuned to brute impulse than he cared
to acknowledge. But would a primitive or Augustan speak
of "relationships"?

In any case, his love for the child didn't appear different
in kind to Caroline. What was so obvious was its sameness.
All love was the same, a desire to gather in and embrace.

Isabel was at her most beautiful the summer she was seven.
With an enviable bronze glow, she resembled an Indian
of the Southwest. Half her length was legs. "A dancer's
legs," one of their friends commented, and Isabel, her legs
stretched out before her on the rug, smiled back shyly, uncomprehending, with missing teeth. Caroline was grateful
for the missing teeth: they represented a visible lapse from
perfection, even if temporary. She didn't like the way the
friend had looked at the child, but told herself she was
being absurd. Isabel was a baby. She liked to wear her long
hair severely tied behind with a ribbon. It swung over her
straight back like a skein of velvet. She winced and groaned
every morning under the hairbrush, while Caroline hard-
ened her heart and brushed on. "You can have it cut if
you want." Isabel shook her head with gentle stubbornness.
"I like it long. Daddy likes it long." She was strong, infatu-
ated with life and her own beauty, spreading an entrancing
glow of goodwill. More than sheer infantile magic—she was
truly good, Caroline believed, the outer beauty an accurate
portrait of the inner. The fluctuations of emotion played
openly on her face in hundreds of tiny gradations in lips
and eyes and color: reading her expression, Caroline felt
she saw through to the purity of nerve and bone. In her
seductive contradictions of innocence and subtlety she was
Ivan all over again, and she was bewitching.

They went, that summer, to an inn in the Berkshires for
two weeks. After a hike in the woods they lay on the large

double bed, Isabel resting between them, holding a hand on either side. Ivan was silent, possibly dozing, while Isabel asked her usual questions and received the usual answers, from a script of unending fascination to her.

"So what do people do when they want to make a baby? Do they say, let's make a baby, just like that?"

"Well, not exactly. It happens in different ways. They usually both know if they want to."

"And then do they just go to bed and do it?"

"Yes."

"Do they have to take off all their clothes?"

"They don't have to, but they usually do."

"It must be so embarrassing. Do they have to be married?"

"No, they don't have to, but most people who have babies are. It's better for the baby that way."

The child suddenly clutched Ivan's arm. He started and blinked. "Let's get married!" she cried.

"What?"

"Let's get married."

"Oh. But I'm already married," he answered her, smiling. This, too, was from the script.

Instantly, with the fleetness of a butterfly, she was stretched out full length on top of him. "Well, let's make a baby anyway."

Ivan put his hands on her shoulders and laughed out loud. "I already made a baby."

"Isabel," said Caroline, "it's hot in here. Go and open the window, please."

Grunting with mild resentment, she climbed off Ivan and did as she was asked. "Anything to get me out of the way," she said good-naturedly.

Caroline blushed. "Come here," she said, smiling. She moved over to make room for Isabel on her right, away from Ivan, circling an arm around her and hugging her close. Her body was soft, immediately yielding. Despite herself, Caroline, too, yielded. "You know I don't want you out of the way." Isabel snuggled into her side. After a while Caroline added, "How did you get so clever?" But no one heard. They had both fallen asleep.

She watched them. They even slept alike, their brows slightly furrowed and their lips, the bowed, exquisitely articulated lips, barely parted. But Ivan, as usual, groped and clung; one leg was flung over her own, a heavy, comforting weight, his fist was pressed into the bend of her waist, and his chin had found her shoulder to lean on. Isabel's sleep was essentially solitary; Caroline might have been a wall or a pillow. She noted with a tinge of nostalgia how Isabel's primitive infant desires were restrained even in sleep: the renounced thumb came to rest gently on her lower lip, pulling it down to reveal the soft inner pink of her mouth.

The child had an unfair advantage, she thought. Isabel did things that she couldn't do. Evenings when she heard the click of the door—and she always heard it first—she raced through the living room to meet Ivan and leap up in his arms. When his hair periodically grew long enough Isabel would tie it back in a rubber band and bring him a mirror to see. He submitted like a ludicrous enchanted lover. Bottom and Titania, Caroline thought, looking on. After her bubble bath Isabel would run out, the huge flowered towel fastened like a sarong, and offer him her small shoulder to smell. Ivan rolled his eyes, sighed, and pretended to swoon.

All little girls did these things, most likely. And she was glad Ivan could yield with whimsical abandon. She loved that in him. In men. Her own father would never have humored her in any such silliness. Caroline could not even recall trying out seductive games. Perhaps all little girls did not do those things, or at least not in quite that beguiling way.

She might attempt things equally beguiling. But the lure of ingenuousness had never been her style, and besides, at thirty-eight years old she could not stoop to copying the wiles of a child. Amazing Grace, another friend called Isabel, after the spiritual. Such a quality descended at random. Useless, mortifying to imitate. Nevertheless, she thought as she watched the child begin to stir and stretch lithely in her sleep, there were a few things she could do that Isabel could not. And recalling those things, she smiled with languor, and a touch of smug, vengeful satisfaction.

Isabel's long lashes fluttered. She smiled up at her mother.

"Did you have a good sleep?" Caroline murmured. She nodded and rubbed her eyes. Caroline glanced over at Ivan. His breathing had changed, quickened. He had rolled off her and lay flat on his stomach. He began to scratch his wrist in his sleep. In five minutes he would be awake.

"Why don't you go take a swim?" she said to Isabel, and sat up to peer through the window at the pool outside. The lifeguard was on his chair and several children around Isabel's size were playing in the shallow water.

"Okay." But she did not move.

"Go on, now." Caroline gave her a gentle nudge. "We'll come out too, in a while. Get your suit on quietly, Daddy's asleep."

As she watched her undress and pull on the one-piece bathing suit she chided herself for being a fool. It was a baby's body. Look at the way she yanked the suit up, shifting from side to side in awkward exaggerated movements. But then, the way she gave herself a final appraising glance in the mirror, flicked her hair off her neck and flung the beach towel over her shoulder . . . . no, that was uncanny. Caroline sighed, discomfort flickering in her chest. "Don't slam the door," she said. "Have fun. And be careful."

The closing of the door, though obediently soft, woke Ivan. He turned, opened his eyes and threw a weighty arm across her. "Mm," he said lazily. "You still here?"

"Obviously."

"Did you sleep?"

"No. I watched you." She ruffled his hair and smoothed it off his forehead.

"Where's Isabel?"

"She went swimming."

"Ah," said Ivan, and put his arms around her, settling his head on her breast as if to sleep again. Then he looked up. "Is the lifeguard there?"

"Yes, I checked."

He settled back on her. "You're soft."

"I know. You're hard." She stroked his back and smiled. She liked the hardness and sometimes wished she were like that. Her mind wandered and blurred, she felt herself falling into sleep. If her body were hard Ivan would not love her in the same way. If she were different in any other aspect he would not, perhaps. She suddenly imagined herself on probation, with all her lovable qualities liable to vanish at any moment, leaving her with no resources. But she smiled—these notions rose from the irrational edge of sleep. The dazed warmth of him drew her in. Then an odd idea struck her, and she was wide awake. Ivan still lay on her breasts and ran a hand aimlessly over her thigh. Her age was against it, but it wouldn't be the first. It was having the first at her age that was most dangerous. She could keep her job—she had gotten tenure two years ago. It would mean more juggling of schedules, more baby-sitters. Money. They could manage it. And they still had the old things in the cellar. Every time friends borrowed them they were returned promptly and in excellent condition. That was almost like an omen. Why not, except for the wear and tear on her own body, before and after? But it would be worth it. Her blood seemed to thicken and slow down, and she felt the heaviness of her years settle softly in her veins—a warning. She shivered; the alien feeling passed. Ivan rolled over on his back. As she regarded him, the idea took root in her body with a frightful tenacity. It seemed a tactic worthy of his invention.

In an instant motion, she sprang up and stretched out full length on top of him. "Let's make a baby," she whispered.

Ivan clasped his arms around her. The bones of his wrists dug low into her back, and her insides pounced in response. "Are you serious, Caroline?"

"Why not? We did so well with the first. I bet we could do it easily this time."

He raised his eyebrows in a parody of shock. "Darling, this is so sudden. I mean . . . Maybe we ought to think about it for a while."

She shifted her weight and reached down to caress him so he would forget the practical objections sprouting in his mind. Raising her head, she could see out the window Isabel at the pool, beautifully poised on the higher of the two diving boards but hesitating, peering with some trepidation down into the blue water. She had only recently learned to swim and had never dived from so high a place. Caroline stiffened with fear, then a sense of immense distance overcame her fright. Let her learn to take risks too. Jump, she thought. Go ahead and jump! As she sent her message she assumed the burden of responsibility for the dive, and accepted the outcome, whatever it might be. With her hand still on Ivan she watched, holding her breath, till Isabel finally jumped on the board, leaped in the air, made of her body a curling arc and plummeted into the water. After a long moment she reappeared yards from the board, shaking water from her face. When she waved at her companions and swam over to join them, Caroline breathed again, heavily, in relief, and turned back to Ivan. She did not tell him about the triumphant dive.

Ivan's face softened, his mouth curved into a smile. She brought her hand up to run a finger over the rim of his lower lip. He rolled her off him gently and began to unbutton his shirt, his fingers fumbling. "Why not?" he said in a low voice. "I don't know what I'm saying," he added after a moment. "This is no way to decide. You must have cast a spell."

"Yes," she whispered in his ear. "I cast a spell." She kissed his lips and reached out to snap the lock on the door. I have him, she thought. Then tears rose in her eyes; she had never intended to be this way with him.

Ivan put his hands on her shoulders. "You're not crying, are you? What is there to cry about?" He had all his clothes off and began on hers. "Come here," he said in a soft urgent tone. "Come on." He stroked her hair. "I'm going to make you very happy."

The second baby was Greta, born when Isabel was nearly eight. There was nothing crooked about Greta's eyes, but in every other respect she was as troublesome a baby as Isabel had been angelic. Caroline and Ivan took turns pacing the floor with her the first year of sleepless nights, and once during what Ivan called the changing of the guard he muttered, "You wanted this. Take her." She took her. She was too numb with exhaustion even to be hurt, and besides, she knew he didn't mean it, he was worn out. Still. They were too old for this. Soon she would be forty. Isabel, who had developed sympathetic insomnia but who read pacifically, curled in a chair with a finger in her mouth, looked up from her book and commented in the offhand manner of her father, " 'They're changing guard at Buckingham Palace—Christopher Robin went down with Alice.' "

"Another great wit. Why don't you just go to bed?" When Isabel ignored her, and Ivan, relieved of his duty, went to the refrigerator to swig ginger ale from the bottle, she cried out over the crying of the baby, "It's two-thirty in the morning and everyone in this household is wide awake! What kind of a crazy place is this? I have to teach a class at nine o'clock. I can't stand it any more!"

"I told you what to do," said Ivan. "Drug her."

She gave in and got a prescription for a sedative. "Now for your sleeping potion, sweetie-pie," she would murmur to Greta each evening, shoving the spoon at her, scraping up any stray drops on her chin and guiding them firmly to her mouth. That took care of the nights, but the days grew worse as Greta grew more mobile. She whipped through the house like a lashing hurricane, not bad-natured, nor frustrated like Koh Ma, but propelled rather by the impersonal fury of the elements. She had physical strength beyond her years, and an appetite for adventure. I didn't need this, Caroline thought. I had my baby already. This was her punishment for trying to deflect Ivan's infatuation. She had interfered with the course of nature and the gods themselves were humbling her.

Indeed her strategy had worked, but in ways she never intended. Ivan doted on them both. He was tired, though, of night feedings and diapers, tired of playing with mashed food and plastic beads, tired of being enlightened and fair-minded. But he was picking the worst possible moment to slacken, for all about them sounded ancestral voices prophesying war. Women, arming unobtrusively for a decade, loosed their primal and most potent of weapons, words. The words sprang from the newspapers, lurked in the mailbox, invaded the bookstores and tumbled from the lips of Caroline's students and friends. She absorbed them avidly. They were a delight to hear, saying things she had known quietly all her life. Once she heard them, she knew she knew them. And even though through circumstance she was raising a family in the conventional way, she still felt herself an anarchist at heart. This rising, at its verbal peak, had gloriously anarchic possibilities.

Reading and listening, she could feel a certain coziness. She had little to complain of, personally. She had always had her work; no one could have stopped her. In two universities she had been the first woman in the mathematics department without thinking much of it, politically, at any rate. She had seen it more as a private feat: sleight of hand, slipping through the eye of the needle. The militant women students in her classes even looked to her as some kind of exemplar, though she felt unworthy. And Ivan did not abuse her for her sex. Ivan, she was gradually discovering, adored, no, esteemed women and girls: the way they thought and spoke and moved and acted and felt. Divorced friends envied her. He was not afraid to wash dishes and he was not afraid to be tender. He was not afraid of hidden teeth in her private passageways. Like Leopold Bloom and unlike most men, he understood or felt what a woman is.

So Caroline went about her business, which was Greta and devastating. Hurricane Greta, a record-breaker. Her life had become incessant labor. Labor at school and labor at home. Somehow there was forever some wretched but consuming task to do, despite the baby-sitters. She had always disliked domestic work, but she dragged herself doggedly from one task to the other without question: they were assigned to her, apparently, by circumstance. When through the death and illness of elderly men, the chairmanship of the department dropped in her lap like a ripe fruit, she felt not honored as she would have years ago, but oppressed. She accepted, certainly; a woman in her position could not refuse. She gave up resting; she would rest in the grave. She lost weight and looked haggard, and cultivated the useful habit of not thinking ahead, or back, or beyond the task at hand, whether laundry or ever-higher-dimensional non-trivial knots.

The family thrived. Isabel was president of the fifth grade, and Greta's powerful arm knocked objects off surfaces, shattered glass. Ivan worked longer hours, writing articles and hustling money for artists. His advice was widely sought; he consulted, he plotted strategies. He was in the prime of life and his energy was boundless. His long hair was in fashion now, and no one wore a tie any more. He marched and rallied, protesting the winding-down war with Greta on his shoulders and Isabel by his side. But she was the anarchist, Caroline thought with some bitterness, and she had no time to protest. Exhilarated by dissent, he came home ready for love. That she hardly minded. That was by far the easiest of her assigned tasks. The thriving literature of sexual discontent gave her guilt pangs, for she felt like those churlish men they complained of: she liked it quick and uncomplicated and with a minimum of talk, playful or soulful. Ivan amorous was like a chef with a gourmet feast in store, whose guests have an appetite only for hamburgers.

He cooked fancy dinners too, once in a while, but he burned the pots. One wintry evening Caroline was attacking the charred grains of rice sticking to the bottom of a pot. Like the anti-war demonstrators, like Ivan himself, they would not be moved. She scrubbed absently, dreaming of a toddlers' play group for Greta, till it struck her that her hand had been oscillating across the bottom of the pot for at least five minutes. Odd, was it not? The motion of the hand, pointless and mechanical, detached from the world of purposeful action, took on an aura of the absurd. Its oscillation, fulfilling some obscure metaphysical arrangement, became sinister. All at once the seeming infinity of her futile motion, of all the tasks she assaulted each day only to see them spring up the next with unremitting life, magnified into the labors of Sisyphus, except Sisyphus, as she remembered Camus pointing out, at least relished his instant of success. And she became, in her own mind, no longer a woman but a symbol, gathering into herself the futile labors of thousands like her. Her head vibrated. Everything she had read and heard seethed and bubbled inside as in a cauldron, and then a crack in the cauldron released a torrent of spewing, accumulated brew, and she ran with dripping hands into the living room, where Ivan sat reading the newspaper and the children played with blocks on the floor.

"Why?" she screamed. "Why am I standing at the sink scrubbing a filthy pot while you're reading the paper? Will you tell me that?"

"But I cooked it. I thought we took turns." He lowered the paper with reluctance.

"What is the use of your cooking," she screamed, "if you burn the pots? Do you know how hard it is to clean a burned pot? You don't, because when I cook I don't burn them. I have never left you a burned pot to clean."

"Throw the pot away. Buy a new pot."

She came closer. She wanted to hit him, he was so calm. The muscles in her right arm tensed to strike, but she was afraid to, in front of Isabel and Greta, who had put down their blocks to watch. "Don't you dare tell me to buy a pot!" She stamped her foot. "I'm sick of your burned pots, and of the whole damned thing."

Ivan got up wearily. "Why don't you go lie down, then? I'll finish the dishes."

"I don't want you to finish the dishes! I want you to explain to me how it came about that I am oppressed by your burned pots, how come I am standing at the sink and you are reading the paper. Is it because you're paid more money for what you do? Is it because you've got a— Is that what gives you the right to burn pots?"

"Now look," said Ivan very loudly. "Now look. I am not oppressing you. I said I'd do the dishes if you're tired."

"I am not tired!" she shrieked. "It's not because I'm tired. Don't you see, this is an oppressive situation."

Ivan threw the newspaper to the floor and lunged forward. "I am not your oppressor!" he yelled.

Together, the children stood up. Isabel turned her head from one to the other, back and forth like a mechanical doll. She had two fingers in her mouth. Greta put her thumb in her mouth and started to wail. Both of them had a demented, mesmerized look.

"I am not your oppressor!" he yelled again, so loud that Caroline stepped back and gasped. She heard Isabel gasp too, above Greta's wails. "Don't call me that! I have never oppressed you or anyone else and I don't intend to. I'll do your fucking dishes but I will not be called an oppressor. You think life is oppressive? I'm just as oppressed as you are. People all over the world are a lot more oppressed than either of us. That's real oppression—you want to try it? It's a political thing. Not burned pots. Did I ever once stop you from doing what you want?" He moved brusquely to pick up Greta but she cowered away from him, howling.

"The political is personal! I mean, the personal is political." She had read that in a magazine the other day. It had seemed profound but now it sounded stupid, with Greta crying and Isabel staring and sucking her finger.

"Don't give me that cant!" Ivan thundered. The hanging asparagus plant in the path of his voice swayed perilously. "I'll do the dishes for the rest of my life if you want, I don't care, but don't give me that nonsense! The personal is just that, *personal!*" He grabbed up the shrieking baby. For a second Caroline thought he would attack Greta, but he tried awkwardly to soothe her. The touch of her quieted him. "Look here, Caroline, I'll do the dishes. We'll eat out. We'll eat pizza. Whatever. I know it's hard. But this is *our* life. Our life is not happening in the pages of some pop magazine. Where are your brains? You're no better than Jerome when you talk like that." He stalked off to the kitchen, carrying Greta.

"Hard!" she yelled after him. "Hard! You don't know what hard is!" She stretched out on the floor. The blood in her head pounded so fiercely she thought it would burst. Isabel knelt beside her. "Are you okay, Mommy?"

"You're old enough to think now. Think, before you ever get married."

From the kitchen, Greta's sobs were subsiding. In a few

moments she appeared, her face red and streaked, with a lollipop in her mouth. Caroline heard running water, the clink of metal against porcelain. Ivan was doing the dishes.

The local nursery school took children at three years old. The day after Greta's birthday party—six toddlers, sugary cake, Scotch neat—Caroline enrolled her. She had a bit of spare time now, and intended to use it for rest. The hangover from the party was prolonged. But on the second day of nursery school she met her old friend the French professor in the university parking lot. She looked beautifully ascetic, he said; she could use some of his brioches. Two days later, still persuasive, he stopped her after class and suggested a drink at his apartment. Caroline was so light-headed knowing Greta would be in school all afternoon and for the next eighteen years that she would have consented to anything.

There was a divorced father who dropped off his child at nursery school the same time she did. He was giddy with relief too. They joked together on the way out like truants. Coffee. Drinks. It seemed inevitable. Ivan had said long ago to use her imagination. Her imagination told her to speed. In dreams reappearing from adolescence she drove convertibles at top speed down endless flights of stairs and woke an instant before the crash. She could do it all if she did it fast. She formed a committee of women in math and the physical sciences, graduate students and younger teachers. A small group. They did not know yet just what their mission would be—there were so many possibilities—but for the moment it was good simply to sit in a room and feel bitter together. She had always wanted to play the flute. Life was brief. She went to the music department for lessons. She raced with the velocity of a whirling dervish from the university to the nursery school, from Isabel's dentist to her ballet classes to student conferences. She could almost be in two places at once. Her comings and goings were a study in complex variables. Mark was teaching that now, as a matter of fact, at Columbia, on her recommendation. He still sent her everything he published and asked for her comments. Touching and unnecessary deference, since, unhindered by any family, his researches had surpassed hers.

Barely eating, she ran on nervous energy and anger, an anger secretive and firmly implanted, like her IUD. Badges of merit, both. She was angry most of all at Ivan: he had no pity for her lot in life. His pity was for starving peasants in far parts of the world, political prisoners in distant cells—he was an avid follower of the news. Caroline too, but what she read in the newspapers abetted her. For the first time she was reading them from cover to cover, compulsively, like a man. Everything fitted in, everything was part of a malevolent ancient scheme. When the courts handed down decisions against abortions and pregnancy benefits, when Bella Abzug was defeated and state legislatures rejected the ERA, she stared at Ivan, reading great classics to his daughters on the floor, with a venomous cold gleam. A natural enemy. Thus did the political become personal.

Taking a shortcut one afternoon down an unfamiliar street, she stopped to admire a huge hairy sheep dog who sniffed at her with curiosity. The youngish owner spoke with animation about how intelligent his dog was: he remembered people he hadn't seen in years. Maybe he had seen Caroline around before. Maybe she had a dog too? No? Well, anyway, maybe she would like to come up to his place, just across the street, for a glass of wine. It surprised her; she had assumed he was homosexual, because of the leather jacket, the tight jeans and boots, the earring and the dog—that was why she talked to him so freely on the street. She glanced at him, at the dog, and at her watch. "I have only thirty-five minutes." "Let's go, then," he said. He was a photographer: there was equipment everywhere—

tripods, black boxes, cameras, rolls of film. Photographs hung all over the walls, mostly group portraits of solemn Mexican and South American Indians. They had a glass of wine. He copulated the way he took pictures, decently enough, with seeming concern for his object but overriding self-absorption. The dog was called Stieglitz. When she hit the street she was horrified at the risk she had taken and dashed home as if pursued. Never again. Still, in a few days she could look back on it detached, and remember the piquant aspects. The world was certainly an amazing place. There was a world beneath the ordinary one, perceptible only to the initiated, where strangers met, signaled, coupled and parted. Was Ivan initiated? They could compare notes. What a pity, indeed, that she could not tell this story to Ivan, for the dog Stieglitz sniffing around the bed, the severe faces of the Indians looking down on them, the tripods like slender dark spectators, possessed just the quality of outlandishness that would entertain him. It came to seem, after a while, that she had done it almost for the satisfaction of telling him, whether to entertain or torment was immaterial. Still, she did not dream of taking such vicious satisfaction. Had she any tears left she would have wept.

Ivan led his own busy life without her, courteous and remote. She felt overlooked. As she whirled from place to place she clung savagely to the notion that it was he who avoided her. She wanted him to give up everything to succor her. He could cajole her and make her stop her running, but he refused. He refused to interfere with the course of her life; he would let her destroy herself, if that was her choice. His obstinate silence was an outrage. Like a starving child clutching an empty bowl, she clutched her resentment to her heart. She dreamed of more obscure ways of tormenting him, but knew in advance that he would not be tormented, or would refuse to show it. She dreamed of poisoning his plants, but when she envisioned herself approaching them, powder in hand, she knew it was beneath her. She dreamed of withholding his mail. She had no wish to read it, only to keep it from him, to deprive him of the world and make him turn to her alone for sustenance. Once she did keep from him an urgent message from work, but when she relented two days later he said it didn't matter, it had been taken care of. Nothing she could do would matter. She seethed. When he went up to bed she drove out alone to midnight movies, and came home to the silent house to sit downstairs in darkness and smoke. She gave him no news of herself, only, scrupulously, of the children, the household. She tested, with a thrill of fear, how far she could go before he would break and try to break her. Before he would leave. She could go vast distances, she found; he was not keeping her, nor was he moving. Long ago, in a different discontent, she had felt like the still point in the whirlpool, and now she was the whirlpool itself, whirling around him. How he liked her in her new guise he did not say. He did not oppress her, that was true. For what he did to her there was no word yet invented; it was something more than ignore, but not quite obliterate. It was patrician, a skillful, unique defense. There were ready labels for what she did to him, though, nothing unique about it, and this too, her own base and limited means, enraged her.

Now and then at night in the dark, briefly unshielded, he would reach out for her. They could do that in silence, old hands, expert at procuring pleasure. Waking in the morning, brittle and tossing, her opening thoughts on making breakfast, packing lunches, planning dinner, the countless ruthless and boring demands of the day, she resumed her anger. But Ivan would smile tentatively, his eyes holding a memory. Only when she stood up and felt the stuff running down her legs did she remember what he was smiling about.

That memory was a luxury she couldn't afford. She washed it away.

Just once, afterwards, lying together, he said, "Why must we be so cruel to each other? Can't we stop this?" She had the satisfaction of refusing an answer. He caressed her again, with gestures of such grace that she tightened every muscle to resist.

"You can't deny," he said in the special voice, nearly forgotten, "that this makes you happy."

"I've never denied it. That's not the point."

But in truth she felt so harassed that she had lost sight of the point altogether.

Looking at herself in the mirror, she wondered if she looked like the callous woman she had become. No, the changes were superficial: she was thinner, her hair was shaggier, her movements more nonchalant and her clothes more expensive—no time to hunt for bargains. She had an air of experience and authority. After Greta, little could frighten her. Ivan had taught her strategies for every situation in life, and she knew how to get along. In topology, there were infinite numbers of looping paths you could take around any given knot, and sometimes when she felt cut loose and freed, she imagined she could travel them all simultaneously. But she knew well that they could be grouped and reduced to a finite number of repeating patterns, all ending at the point where they began. She had become an exaggeration, she felt, a parody of a certain kind of driven woman. The French professor, whom she saw once in a while, said that in the last year or so she had become a very beautiful woman. An impressively beautiful woman. She liked hearing it. He said it in three languages. Ivan rarely said things like that. She laughed with the French professor and said, "Oh, you just like them aging and gaunt." But she would never trust a flatterer.

At home there was no need to talk about separation or divorce or breaking up the family. They were separate enough. When their hours did not coincide, she and Ivan left each other notes, informative like the memos of business partners, often witty and stylized, on some days even affectionate. Coming in late one night and finding him asleep contentedly on his side of the bed, a note on her pillow—please get him up at seven—Caroline thought, He must have someone. He wouldn't go for weeks at a stretch without it. And the sight of him, the classic lines so pure and harmless in sleep, gave her a terrible pang of nostalgia, and of love, unaccustomed. She missed him bitterly. Her anger, stiff and heavy, was the oppressor, a mercenary's suit of armor. Did she have to be angry too at the burden of waking him? At the casualness of the request? She was sated with anger. She would wake him. She tossed from dawn on anyway, and he knew it. Naturally she looked no different in the mirror. Naturally, because it was only the center that had dissolved, the living part, that once had grown layers and striations of color from exposure, had been lashed by weather and sent out tendrils of connection, to him, and that she had permitted to be crushed to nothing, by politics. The center was empty and longing for him. Wherever she was, however she fled him, she was thinking of him, a bondage more constraining than love.

On a Saturday afternoon in early June she came home from her office pulsing with energy, and flung down her book bag. She had finished the most resistant section of a paper she was scheduled to deliver at a conference, then stopped to visit the French professor, who gave her coffee and the inevitable brioches. The aroma of honeysuckle rising from the hedges into the lush spring air had encircled her all the way home. Now she would see to the children. Isabel, who was almost thirteen, was recovering from chicken pox, and Greta would break out at any moment. On the living room floor, Ivan, wearing his glasses, sat cross-legged, reading aloud with the book on his ankles. Isabel and Greta lay stretched out before him, rapt like statues. They looked up at her and smiled but didn't speak. There was a passionate hush in the air, of people holding their breath in unison with anticipation and wondrous dread.

" 'What were the use of my creation, if I were entirely contained here?' " said Ivan, his husky voice rolling with sonorous urgency. Greta's thumb rested inert between her front teeth. " 'My great miseries in this world have been Heathcliff's miseries, and I watched and felt each from the beginning: my great thought in living is himself. If all perished, and *he* remained, *I* should still continue to be; and if all else remained and he were annihilated, the universe would turn to a mighty stranger: I should not seem a part of it.' " He paused and glanced at Caroline as though to welcome her, for she had stretched out on the floor with the children, to listen. " 'My love for Linton is like the foliage in the woods: time will change it, I'm well aware, as winter changes the trees. My love for Heathcliff resembles the eternal rocks beneath: a source of little visible delight, but necessary. Nelly, I *am* Heathcliff! He's always, always in my mind: not as a pleasure, any more than I am always a pleasure to myself, but as my own being. So don't talk of our separation again: it is impracticable.' "

He stopped, releasing his audience. There was a moment of ardent silence. Ivan took out a handkerchief, blew his nose, and surreptitiously wiped his eyes with his fist. Isabel turned to Caroline.

"Mom, why are you crying? It's only a story."

"I can't help it. Stories always make me cry. Look, Greta is crying too." She put her arm around Greta and drew her close; her childish eyes, shining with sorrow, streamed. "Do you understand it?" she asked.

Greta shook her head no, and wept.

Ivan took off his glasses and rubbed his eyes again. He stretched out his legs and stretched his arms towards the ceiling. Their eight legs, elongated on the rug like chaotic vectors, were identically clad in blue jeans. They all wore cotton T-shirts. The four of them, she thought, were like members of a primitive clan, bound by the markings of hallowed tradition.

"You read so beautifully," she said to Ivan. "You make it real."

"Well, I have good material. And you came in at the right moment."

She couldn't look at him. "I wish you would read to me sometime."

"You do? But you're so busy. You're always dashing somewhere."

"I could make time to hear you read like that." If only he would read to her like that she would not need to whirl any longer. That would content her. "My love for Heathcliff resembles the eternal rocks beneath." Yes, that would do. It transcended the political, and even the personal.

A year of kindergarten had a calming effect on Greta, so that Caroline no longer woke at sunrise with the apprehension of disaster—would they survive this day? The house was not the prison of perpetual dangers, as in Greta's earliest years. As though she and the child were reflections of each other's inner state, Caroline's vision unblurred as Greta calmed: Ivan was not responsible for social atrocities. It was hard to say who was responsible; that was the problem. Everyone had an historical alibi. The political was so impersonal.

Gradually she slowed down; the pulses that used to beat on the surface of her skin like the vibrations of an itchy serpent—the amused French professor's image—disappeared. In a delicate manoeuvre, she slipped out from under the skin of her anger to laze in the back yard sun. With the relentlessness of truth, the dispatches about women and men kept coming at her in all their dissonant clamor. She tried to cleave to their truth but scrape away the fury it came wrapped in like a layer of static. That was an even trickier manoeuvre, requiring some imagination.

With Ivan she lived in the uneasy balance of truce, like ancient, bickering neighbor nations of common descent, common language, and common perversity. There might never be a lasting peace, but the injuries seemed smaller in scale, and in any case they were even. He was the more magnanimous power; as her malice ebbed, it was he who found the means to approach with the olive branch. More magnanimous, or politically astute? She didn't pursue the question.

There were times, especially when Greta relapsed into peril, that she cried out to herself, No, the cause is just! And she wanted to flee. But you could serve a just cause insanely, she remembered. Flight was no service. It was worse than being a closet anarchist. The cause *was* just, but were their lives not their own, and a cause more just? Or simply more precious? She was full of these contradictions and qualifications. Her life was so riddled with ambiguity that any path she chose was a betrayal of something. But she was hanging on, though it was hardly what she had expected.

Like Caroline, Greta was still intermittently alarming. She tugged at a picture book wedged tightly in the bookcase supported by tension poles, and the entire structure collapsed. Luckily she covered her head with both hands while scrambling out. At the university swimming pool while Caroline's back was turned, she wandered onto the high diving board, pranced, and fell in. Luckily, Ivan had taught her to swim a bit, early on. And one night with Ivan and Caroline out at the movies and Isabel on the phone with a friend, she dragged a ladder to the center of her bedroom, unscrewed the burnt-out light bulb and screwed in a new one. She had forgotten to turn off the switch. Startled by the sudden light and heat, she fell off the ladder, breaking a finger. Isabel found a neighbor to drive them to the emergency room, where the family was known. Looking at the splint when she returned from the movies, Caroline grieved that this accident was her fault because she used to lecture her daughters about self-sufficiency: they must not get into the habit of waiting for Ivan to make simple repairs.

Greta's most terrifying venture was the fault of a feverish imagination, and occurred the summer they spent packing. Caroline and Ivan were tired of their small university town. They wanted action, noise, flurry. Without saying so aloud, they each wanted to leave the scene of remembered ugly spells. Ivan had received a call from New York in the spring: he was offered a tantalizing place at the Metropolitan Museum. And the City University needed someone with a background in topology and knot theory. An available qualified woman was beyond their wildest hopes. She could embody affirmative action. Like Yeats's Anne Gregory, she wished they could love her for herself alone and not her yellow hair. But not even Ivan could manage that. Yeats said only God could do it. So they sold the house in which they had built up equity, and in their bedroom, stripped prints from the walls. Standing on the ladder, Caroline heard strange sounds from the other side of the wall, Greta's room. They were rhythmic, repetitious sounds, like an incantation. Greta was in there with her dearest friend, a tractable boy named Harold, who camped at their house weekends from dawn to dusk.

"I have a funny feeling," she said to Ivan, climbing down. "I think I'd better go see what she's up to."

Ivan no longer laughed at her funny feelings. He had come to the conclusion that Greta was the true anarchist—nothing could restrain the public unfurling of her private identity. He laid down his screwdriver and came along. Caroline pushed open Greta's door.

The children sat on the floor facing each other. Greta held a long bread knife in her right hand and chanted, "This vow will seal our kinship true, Blood of me and blood of you." Blood oozed slowly from her left index finger. She was reaching for Harold's right hand, which he sat on. "Come on, Harold, it doesn't really hurt."

Ivan grabbed the knife out of her fist. Caroline slumped against the door frame with her hand pressed against her heart. She felt very old. Too old.

"I wouldn't hurt him," Greta protested to Ivan. "It's because we're moving, and I want us to be blood brothers. He's my best friend."

Ivan squeezed her finger and wiped it with his handkerchief. "You could have chopped a finger off, do you know that! This is going to need iodine! And Harold! Don't you know any better?"

Harold hung his head and sucked an edge of his polo shirt.

"What was that you were saying?" asked Caroline.

"This vow will seal our kinship true, Blood of me and blood of you."

"And where did you hear that? On one of those crummy TV shows?"

"I made it up."

"Don't give me stories. Where did you hear it?"

Greta's eyes filled with tears of injury. "I saw them do it on a TV show, but I made up the poem myself."

"Don't you ever open a kitchen drawer again!" Caroline shouted. "Don't even go in the kitchen!"

Isabel ambled in. These days she affected a sullen, slinking walk which suited her narrow body very well. She was nearly as tall as her mother. In one languid hand she held *Jane Eyre*, a finger keeping her place. "What is all the commotion? Oh, hi there, Harold."

"Your sister was performing an ancient ritual," said Ivan, brandishing the knife. "She was making Harold a blood brother. Welcome him to the family."

"Oh God," said Isabel, averting her eyes. "That child is incorrigible. I shudder to think what will become of her."

"Oh, cut it out," said Caroline. "Incidentally, Isabel, I have an idea. Do you know what you might do this summer?"

"What might I do?"

"You might teach Greta to read. I think she's ready. I'm sure you'd be an excellent teacher."

"I wouldn't mind," said Isabel, glancing down at her sister as if from a great height, "but I doubt that her attention span would be sufficient."

"Yes it would!" cried Greta.

"I want to read too," said Harold.

"I'll teach you also," said Isabel, "but only if you stop sucking on shirts."

In adolescence the once-gracious Isabel was proud and haughty. She found her parents deficient in many ways, notably in self-discipline, a charge which pained though they laughed with irony. "She should only know," Ivan said. Caroline felt sorry for him—he had drunk up the adoration so thirstily. They joined forces to defend each other against Isabel's lucid critiques: what could they possibly understand of passion and commitment, the conflicts between the actual and the ideal, the fire in the blood? Their speeches for the defense were mutually touching: they had forgotten, in all their strife, that they thought so well of each other. Greta was friendly still, but in the territory of adventure she had staked out as her own, they knew they had no place, unless that of the occupying militia. For solace they turned back, no longer young, but powerful, to each other.

By the time they had lived in New York for two years, almost everyone they knew had been divorced. It was like a marathon, thought Caroline, in which all dropped out but the most tenacious runners, panting and sore. Ivan had become an accomplished runner, in fact, and hoped to be ready for the Central Park Marathon in a year or two. When he went out in his white shorts and blue shoes these days, she did not work herself up with self-indulgent fantasies, or even think much about it. Nor did she ever run with him—she hated fads, and found him strangely guilty of a lapse in taste—but she did dance exercises on the hard wood floor instead, listening to music. She did not accompany him to the galleries either, in his quest for enduring beauty, and he did not go to the Mozart festivals, to which she bought subscriptions and took along friends or Isabel. She still disliked professional parties where she was expected to appear in the role of Ivan's wife, but she went and performed because she knew he needed her there; he alluded proudly to her esoteric work and she smiled esoterically. Occasionally on the way home she ranted her resentments and he listened, driving calmly and very fast, secure in the knowledge that eventually, like a record, she would run down. For her part, she was glad to stop asking him to math department gatherings, where the jokes were exclusive and abstruse, and he was bored. All parties were haunted by the ghosts of missing persons. Everyone mingled with everyone else—there were few firmly packaged husbands and wives as there had been in Boston—and Chantal's living arrangements would hardly be considered eccentric.

What they did together was gossip with old friends and attend assemblies of protest. They were congenital protesters, they finally acknowledged, and politics could be relied on indefinitely for the necessary evils. Caroline still would not throw a bomb into the stock exchange, even at night when no one was there, but she had come round secretly to hope that someone with fewer scruples would. And they went ice skating and to the movies, especially Italian movies, which they loved indiscriminately. She was able, at last, to appreciate movies about the ambivalences of power, and Ivan had developed a taste for the grand simplicities of passion. He read to her sometimes, feelingly, in bed, from old and great tales of love and betrayal and sacrifice. She listened entranced. But when they made love they had to keep their cries and laughs down, because Isabel, sizzling with energy, prowled the apartment till all hours.

This weekend Isabel was on a class trip to Washington, and Greta had gone straight from school to a friend's house, where she would stay till Sunday. "Please be careful, sweetie," Caroline urged in the morning, packing her off. "So they'll want to invite you again." After the Friday classes, to savor her solitude she lay on the floor rereading *The Portrait of a Lady*. It was not the same as when she had read it the first time, when she, too, stood on the brink of life, peering into its dangers and delights and temptations. Then she had brought to the book a corresponding eagerness. Now she brought a wry wisdom. And a touch of envy, also, as well as of relief, for James's Isabel would be forever young and forever susceptible. She was luckier than that valiant Isabel, she reflected. The self-absorbed aesthete she had married was good, not evil. And at that notion, as if on cue, Ivan unlocked the front door and came striding down the hall whistling the tune from Rome, which he always whistled off key, just missing the parabolic curves of the melody. She put the book aside and lay flat on her back, viewing him upside down. He stood at her head waving a bottle of champagne in each hand.

"Are we alone at last?" he greeted her.

"We are alone. What's that for?"

"To celebrate. I brought two. One for before and one for after. Don't go away, I'll put them on ice."

When he returned she said, "Did I forget some great occasion?"

He bent over her. "Oh, you're such a stuffy old professor, Caroline. We're celebrating being alone. A hundred years of solitude. Would you ever have imagined . . . I mean, I'd sell my soul for a weekend."

"Oh, Ivan." She put her hands in his hair. Only a little thinner—a diminishing arithmetic progression. At this rate it would last. Maybe his father had been right about the brushing.

He was fumbling at her clothes, looking for bare skin, which, wide awake, he quickly found. "Or maybe . . . Oh," he sighed, "Caroline, baby. You're all warm."

"Yes. I was waiting for you," she whispered in his ear. "Just for this. Maybe what?"

"Maybe we should have them both after."

"Oh yes . . . Oh yes . . . That's a better idea. But, Ivan, love. Let's go to bed. Because . . . the floor . . . is so hard."

"You never did like hard floors, did you?"

"Ah, you think you know everything I like?"

"I think I do, mm-hm. Don't I, now?"

"Well, sure, that's very nice, but what if I developed . . . oh . . . new predilections?"

"I would soon discover them. You have no escape."

She closed her eyes with a feeling of levitation, but then let go of him. "Really, let's go to bed. Or it will be too late, and my back will hurt."

"But how will we get there? I don't want to move, Caroline. I'm so comfortable here."

"That's because you're not lying on something hard. It's only a little way, love. Come on, get up, I'll help you. That's it. Lean on me. No, I can't carry you, though. You're too big. And how can I walk when you do that? Save that for later. You're too much."

"Thank you, ma'am. That was a fine trip. A little bumpy. All right, here's the bed, so no more of your delaying tactics. Let's have the goods."

"Well, if I have to go through with it, I'll resign myself."

"I'm afraid so. Now don't be shy, sweetheart. I know you're very shy about these things. This won't take more than a little while, and it's completely painless if you just relax."

"For Chrissake, Ivan, I'm all relaxed already! How long are you going to keep this up?"

"Oh, you'd be surprised, baby. Now, why do you keep on laughing? I never saw a woman laugh so much at such a serious moment. How do you expect to get this done laughing like a loon? Sober up."

After, Ivan got up and brought the champagne and glasses back to bed. He popped the cork, the cold wine steamed, and he caught it in time, expertly. They drank.

"This is good," Caroline sighed. "It's so hot in here. I'm burning up. And it's only June."

"Oh, hot flashes?"

"That's not funny, because pretty soon it'll be the real thing. I'm getting on."

"You're complaining. I'm half a century old, and do you realize that all my life I've been surrounded by women? That's just what I was afraid of."

"Well, you've borne your fate bravely. Like a man."

"Thanks a lot. What I mean is, all my attachments . . . all my great loves have been women."

Besides the three of them, she wondered, who else? "So be bisexual. It's never too late. See if I care."

He moved away and slammed his empty glass on the night table. "Why do you have to be that way? Why do you have to reduce things? I'm trying to tell you something serious."

"I'm sorry. You're awfully touchy, you know? I do take you seriously. This business of being flippant to avoid . . . I picked it up from you. You're the original avoider."

"Why don't you pick up my better traits?"

"Well, maybe I have, also. All right, go on. I'm really listening. All your great loves have been women." She poured them both more champagne. If he intended to confess anything, she wanted to be fortified.

"I mean, not things or ideas or causes," he said morosely. "This is a certain sort of life, that's all. Limited. Private. There are other ways to live."

"I know. We got caught up. But you would never have been a lover of things or ideas anyway. You see through everything. That's why I like you."

He moved closer and laid a heavy arm across her. "You're the only one who stayed with me. Everything else moved on." He chuckled. "You're a living example of perseverance. It must come from untangling all those knots."

So it was victory by default? This time she considered her words carefully. "Isabel will be back to you in a few years."

Ivan smiled. "And you've grown so discreet, too. All the Henry James. No, it will never be the same, with Isabel. And Greta—to Greta I don't think we're quite real. So there's only you, Caroline."

It was true: no one rushed to greet him at the door any more. Greta sat absorbed in her books, and Isabel was far beyond such antics.

He rested his head on her chest. "I can hear your heart."

"What is it saying?"

"Well." He paused. "Your heart, as we know, is topological."

"Oh, is it?" she smiled.

"Yes. It's saying, 'A perfect circle is a trivial knot.' "

Her eyes flicked open. "Hey, that's not bad. Not bad at all. You have possibilities."

"Did you think I could have hung around this long without learning anything?"

She watched him as he lay sprawled across her. Outwardly he had not changed very much. He had never turned into the middle-aged monster she dreaded. That was partly luck. The circumstantiality of her life sent a shiver of mortality though her. Lying on her chest as if he belonged there was a person who had aroused her at a party over twenty years ago on a sunny afternoon when she was lonely and slightly drunk, and so—her life. Only one turn round, and hers was more than half passed. Had it been different weather or different wine, had he not taken her immediately into those dark recesses to show her a she-wolf . . . That she loved him in a way that was appalling, that things about him over which he had little control—ways of seeing and of speaking, ways of being—exerted a control over her, she accepted now as a fact of life, neither loathsome nor lovely. She could confront it with detachment, like other facts about herself. There might easily have been other facts in its place, equally intransigent, more or less dense with possibility. But there would not be. Or was it still too soon to say?

Ivan sat up and tipped the bottle over her glass; only a

few drops came out. "There's more inside," he said. "Do you want to get really looped?"

"Sure. We're on our own. I'll get it this time. Let me open one."

"Ha! Did you ever open a bottle of champagne? It's an art. It can't be done sloppily."

"I'm not a slob! At the last two department parties I did it. It's not beyond my powers." With the French professor too, on several occasions that she recalled quite vividly, but she could not say that.

"I'm sure it's not, but I'll do it anyway." He got out of bed and headed towards the kitchen.

She leaped up and followed. "Not this time, sweetheart. I want to open a bottle. Fair's fair." She chased him and overtook him in the living room, and they raced to the kitchen. Ivan got there first, flung the refrigerator open and seized the champagne. He laughed exultantly and waved it aloft. Caroline yanked his arm down and grabbed the neck of the bottle. Their four hands slipped and grappled on the dewy surface, tugging above their heads.

"Come on, baby, let go."

"Never! Why don't you?"

"If only I had a free hand," gasped Ivan, "oh, what I would do to you."

"I don't need a hand. I could destroy you with a knee."

"Your loss," he jeered.

Then by a common impulse, at the same instant they both yielded. The bottle fell from its height to the hard tiles. Pieces of glass bounced like a starburst. Sweet-smelling foam streamed onto the kitchen floor, and blood flowed from Ivan's ankle.

"Look what the hell you've done!" he shouted. "You're so damn perverse!"

"And you're so damn stubborn!" she shouted back. "Sit down and let me look at that. And watch your bare feet."

"You watch your bare ass." But he sat.

Ivan's blood dripped into the rills and puddles of champagne that eddied out on the floor, making the two of them into an island. The blood slid in sinuous arcs that quickly dissolved and turned the liquid a pale, effervescent pink.

Caroline examined his ankle. "It's not as bad as it looks. A little cut and a lot of blood. Have no fear, you'll run again."

"Look at this disgusting mess," he muttered. "Senseless. Too bad there's no ship."

She dabbed at his ankle with a paper napkin and turned it toward the light. Something glinted. "Hold it, Ivan. Sit still. You have a bit of glass in there."

"Oh, terrific. We don't even need Greta around to have a calamity. And you used to worry when I disappeared in the park. It's much more dangerous at home with you."

She stroked his leg. "Stop it," she said softly. "Will you stop being so angry? We both did it."

"Oh, all right." He took a deep breath. "But will you take the glass out of my leg? If it's there. I can't see it."

"Your eyes," she said, shaking her head. She bent over his ankle and picked out the sliver, not half an inch long. She held it for a moment in the palm of her hand, then lifted it and looked into his eyes. He looked back uncomprehending at first, then slowly he smiled and leaned back, waiting. It was the smile that had first undone her, that made him ingenuous, accessible. His eyes shone a brighter green.

She sliced a careful line on the tip of her index finger. Blood oozed. "This vow will seal our kinship true . . ."

"You are . . . not quite the usual article," whispered

Ivan. He put his hands on her bare shoulders. "I knew when I first saw you, in that setting, you would be . . . I don't know what it is. Wild."

She winked and rubbed her bleeding finger on Ivan's cut ankle. "Blood of me and blood of you."

He kissed her finger, and then her mouth. "But," he said, "I still think I could have opened it better. I have more experience."